At First Sight

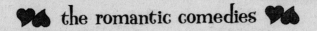
the romantic comedies

At First Sight

CATHERINE HAPKA

Simon Pulse

New York London Toronto Sydney

SIMON PULSE
An imprint of Simon & Schuster Children's Publishing Division
1230 Avenue of the Americas, New York, NY 10020
First Simon Pulse paperback edition April 2010
Copyright © 2010 by Catherine Hapka
All rights reserved, including the right of reproduction in whole or in part in any form.
SIMON PULSE and colophon are registered trademarks of Simon & Schuster, Inc.
For information about special discounts for bulk purchases, please contact Simon & Schuster Special Sales at 1-866-506-1949 or business@simonandschuster.com.
The Simon & Schuster Speakers Bureau can bring authors to your live event. For more information or to book an event contact the Simon & Schuster Speakers Bureau at 1-866-248-3049 or visit our website at www.simonspeakers.com.
Designed by Ann Zeak
The text of this book was set in Garamond 3.
Manufactured in the United States of America
10 9 8 7 6 5 4 3 2 1
Library of Congress Control Number 2009934852
ISBN 978-1-4169-9885-3
ISBN 978-1-4169-9886-0 (eBook)

At First Sight

One

My best friend, Britt, was madly in love. Again.

"OMG!" she said with an adorable giggle, fluttering her long eyelashes at the cute guy in the kung fu T-shirt and Abercrombie cargoes. "I can't believe you go to Greenleaf High. I've always said Greenleaf has the cutest guys in the entire state of Maryland. Right, Lauren?" She waved one hand in my direction without breaking eye contact with Greenleaf Guy. "By the way, this is my best friend, Lauren Foley."

My introduction barely warranted a cursory glance, nod, and mumbled "hi" from the object of Britt's affection. Or maybe that should be "affliction." See, Britt has a lifelong case of severe boycrazyitis. One I seriously doubted would be cured anytime soon.

"Lauren's the one who convinced me to come over and say hi to you," Britt continued, tilting her head up at Greenleaf Guy. "Usually I'm totally shy about talking to cute guys."

It was all I could do not to burst out laughing at that one. Britt, shy with guys? Hardly. She's pretty much fearless, not to mention completely lacking in the capacity for shame or embarrassment. Everyone says that's why guys are drawn to her like dogs to a fire hydrant. Not that she isn't cute—she is. But even if a guy doesn't notice her pixielike face, her perfect skin, or her great legs, she makes damn sure he notices *her*.

To keep from blowing her cover, I wandered off a ways and pretended to be fascinated by a display case showing an astronaut in full bubble-headed regalia. Britt and I, along with the rest of the junior class of Potomac Point High and those of like half the other schools in our county, were at the National Air and Space Museum at the Smithsonian in Washington, D.C.

Why, you ask? Good question. The answer is, we were being subjected to a ridiculously lame multischool field trip sponsored by some science foundation.

Not that I have anything against the Smithsonian. In fact, I kinda like it, especially the First Ladies' gowns at the American History museum. But spaceships and black holes and airplanes? So not my thing.

I watched Britt and the guy in the reflection of the display case. I saw her toss her short blond hair around—a patented Britt flirting move. It worked. The guy stepped a little closer, his hands twitching as if he was dying to touch her.

Then I saw Britt glance around with an adorably furtive expression. She reached into her purse and pulled out BBB. That's a nickname I came up with; it stands for Beloved BlackBerry. It could just as easily stand for Britt's Bodacious Bestie, BlackBerry Baby, or Beautiful Best Buddy. Get the picture? She loves the thing.

Anyway, PDAs, cell phones, and all other electronic devices were strictly verboten on this trip, but Britt has never been that good at following the rules. One of the numerous things she and I *don't* have in common. So she and the guy bent over the BlackBerry, her slim fingers flying over the tiny keys.

My gaze drifted away. I knew what came next. Britt would enter the guy's name and number into her log, then add him as a friend on Facebook. I wondered if he'd be shocked when he logged on and saw that his "shy" new acquaintance had like forty gazillion other FB friends, mostly guys. . . .

As I amused myself with that thought, I found myself staring at the spaceman in front of me. The bubble-headed look was a little retro for my taste. I automatically started redesigning the space suit, adding a touch of color here, streamlining the fabric there . . .

See, that's my thing. Fashion. I love clothes. Most of my daydreams revolve around becoming an international fashion icon, showing up on runways from New York to Milan with my daringly original designs, shocking and amazing the fashion elite with my talent and creativity.

Not that I would ever have the guts to actually *do* anything like that. Britt is always on my case about being too cautious. She wants me to actually create every over-the-top outfit I sketch, no matter how wild or weird, and then wear it to school just to see what happens. But unlike her, I'm not a just-to-see-what-happens kind of girl. I prefer to test the waters first.

My gaze returned to the reflective surface of the display case, but this time I was staring at myself. My ordinary hazel eyes. My perky but unexceptional nose. And my best feature, my long, thick, wavy dark hair. If I ever tried shaking it around like Britt did with hers, would it have the same mesmerizing effect on guys? Or would I just end up looking like I had a gnat in my ear? Thoughts like that never seemed to occur to Britt at all, but my brain produced them so freely that I sometimes wondered if it was a medically diagnosable condition.

"Listen up, people!" Mr. Feldman's voice rang out across the museum. He's the head of PPH's science department and actually a pretty cool guy, despite teaching my least favorite subject and being possibly the worst-dressed high school teacher of all time. And if you've ever been to high school, you know that's saying something. "It's time for a fascinating look at the work scientists do behind the scenes here at the Air and Space Museum," he said in his nasal voice.

"Potomac Point and East Elm students, please come with me. March!"

A couple of other teachers called out similar orders, directing the other schools to their own areas. The horde of high schoolers filling the museum's airy atrium started dividing itself into smaller groups like some giant amoeba splitting into different parts, and I started preparing myself for more tedium. See, wandering around on guided tours of the museum's endless array of flying machines, as boring as it was, was actually the fun part. In between, we were stuck listening to a bunch of lectures about stuff like quarks and wind shear and who knew what else. Speaking as someone who can barely stay awake in science class, I couldn't think of a suckier way to spend my day.

Britt bounced over to join me as I started shuffling along with the crowd following Mr. Feldman. "What did you think of Trent?" she demanded eagerly. "Isn't he the awesomest? Talk about love at first sight!"

"Sort of like the other three guys you've fallen in love with so far today?" I paused, feigning deep thought with one finger to my chin. "Or was it four? I've lost count."

"Mock me if you wish, Lauren," she retorted. "Trent might very well be the love of my life. I would hope my best friend might at least *try* to be happy for me."

"If you make it to your two-week anniversary with that guy, I'll be ecstatic, trust me," I told her as we filed into some backstage part of the museum. "Not to mention shocked."

Britt stuck out her tongue at me. We had to stop talking for a while as some dude started droning on about the scientific method. Or something like that. I had to mentally redesign not only his wardrobe— I put him in classic dark pinstripes with a floral tie for a splash of color—but also those of everyone else in the room just to keep from dozing off.

Seventeen hours later, we were finally released back into the main part of the museum. Okay, maybe it wasn't quite that long. But it felt like it. Most of the other schools hadn't yet emerged from their torture chambers—er, lectures—so the place had a weekday-morning-at-the-mall sort of feel. Not that I'd ever have the guts to skip class to go shopping, of course.

"So are you saying you don't believe

Trent and I are meant to be?" Britt asked, picking up right where we'd left off.

"I'm saying I don't believe in love at first sight." We'd had this same discussion so many times it was practically scripted. "There's no way you can tell if you're going to hit it off with someone just by looking at him."

"Trust me, babe. I can tell."

Britt sank down onto a free bench, casting an appraising eye toward a good-looking artsy type standing nearby looking at one of the displays. When a Goth girl with a nose ring came over and wrapped one skinny arm around him, stretching up to lick his earlobe, Britt shrugged and returned her gaze to me.

"It's called sparks," she informed me. "And I know them when I feel them."

"Right. *Every* time you feel them." I smirked. "And sorry, but I'm just not willing to believe that sparks and raw animal attraction equal true love."

She grinned back at me. "Don't knock it till you try it. Your love life could stand a little more raw animal attraction."

"If you say so." It was a familiar exchange. Britt wasn't trying to be mean about my love life—or relative lack thereof. I knew she truly didn't understand how I could be content waiting for romance to come to me rather than rushing out, grabbing it with both hands, and checking out its butt, like she did.

But that was mutual. I didn't really get the whole "sparks" thing, either. I mean, sure, I sometimes felt a flutter of hormones when I saw a cute guy walking through the mall or something. Same flutter I got when I saw a hot actor on TV or up on the movie screen. That silly flutter just didn't seem like a solid basis for a relationship to me.

One of the other school groups emerged from their lecture. A pair of beefy jock types wearing varsity jackets wandered past where we were sitting, ribbing each other loudly about football. Or maybe baseball. Something with balls, anyway. Britt sized them up as they passed our bench.

"Any sparks?" I teased.

She tore her gaze away from the guys and made a face at me. "Very funny. You know I'm totally committed to Trent."

For about two and a half seconds she managed to keep a straight face. Then she cracked up. So did I.

"Seriously, though, Lauren," she said, once we got control of ourselves, "I wish you'd let yourself go and just believe in love for a change."

"I do believe in love. Just not love at first sight."

"Okay. But why not at least give the sparks thing a try? What could it hurt?"

"Oh, I don't know. Dying of embarrassment probably hurts at least a little bit."

"You wouldn't actually die, you know," she said.

"I know. I'd just *want* to. And then I'd have to go into the witness protection program, and I'd probably end up living in, like, Iowa or somewhere, with a family who eats mac and cheese for dinner every night and wears polyester. And that would be truly painful."

"Very creative," she said. "But you're avoiding the question. Why not try it just once?"

"That's not the point. I'm not like you. I don't get sparks."

"You say it like it's a disease, Ms. Uptight."

"I'm not uptight. Just sane," I shot back automatically.

She gave me a look. As usual every thought in her head was written all over her face, and I knew she didn't really believe me. She thought I was just holding back, not letting myself go for it with guys the way she did. But it wasn't like that. I truly didn't get the sparks she was always claiming to feel with Mr. Right–du-Jour. Or du-Hour. It just hadn't worked for me like that in the past. I'd only had a couple of semiserious boyfriends in my entire life, and in both cases they'd started out as friendships that slowly grew into more.

"Look, you deal with guys and romance and stuff your way, and I deal with it in mine," I told her.

"You mean Jason and that guy from the pool?" She wrinkled her nose. "Please. Hanging out with a guy for ages until one night you stay up too late watching scary movies and accidentally start making out hardly qualifies as romance."

She made it sound so sordid. And worse yet, so dull.

"Jason and I were together for almost six months," I reminded her.

"And then what happened? Things got boring and fizzled out. Real romantic."

"It still beats your two-week record for a relationship lasting," I retorted.

She grinned. "Okay, touché or whatever. But listen, seriously? This trip is the perfect time to scope out some fresh meat. There are tons of cute guys here from other schools, so if you do embarrass yourself, you'll never have to see them again. But it's way more likely they'll be so blown away by your gorgeous face, superhot bod, and incredible hair that you'll end up with more dates than me."

"If I do, I'll probably end up in *Guinness World Records*."

"Come on, I'm serious." Britt reached into her purse for her favorite MAC lipstick. "What's the worst that could happen? And it's not like you're all fascinated by this spaceship stuff anyway."

I glanced around at the rocket-type artifacts surrounding us. "True. But I'm happy just to sit here and wallow in boredom. You go ahead and scope away to your heart's content. I'll watch and take notes."

"No you won't." After reapplying, she capped her lipstick and dropped it back in her purse. "You'll just watch, and then make fun of me later."

"You know me so well."

My tone was light, but she responded with uncharacteristic seriousness. "Right. And I know you well enough to know you deserve to find the perfect guy. All it takes is a little effort, a little risk."

"Well, maybe if I ever actually run into someone who's worth the . . ."

My voice trailed off before I could finish the sentence. Because I'd just spotted the most jaw-droppingly gorgeous guy I'd ever seen.

Two

He was leaning against a wall across the way looking just as bored as I felt. Tall and dark-haired and sort of rumpled, but in a cute way, wearing faded jeans and a concert T-shirt. He was drumming on his knees and nodding rhythmically as if hearing music in his head—a musician, maybe?

I felt a weird little rush. Like all the blood in my entire body suddenly decided it needed to be somewhere *else* in my body. And then there was my head. There was some pinging going on up there. I'm not sure how else to describe it. Just . . . pinging.

"Check it out," I whispered, more to myself than to Britt, as my gaze wandered back to the T-shirt. I'd recognized the logo right away. "He must be into Maybe There Is a Beast."

Britt followed my gaze. "The Beast? They're, like, your favorite local band ever!" she hissed. "You should totally go talk to him!"

She had that excited glint in her eye that meant she was getting revved up about this already. I had to reel her in before she did something embarrassing. Embarrassing for *me*, not her, obviously. But for a second I couldn't say anything. I was still feeling that weird rushing and pinging. It was kind of distracting. Could these be the sparks Britt was always talking about?

A sharp poke in the ribs brought me out of my stupor. "Go over and talk to him!" Britt urged in a stage whisper so loud I was pretty sure they could hear it on Jupiter even without the help of any of the scientific space gizmos currently surrounding us.

The guy was still drumming on his knees, seemingly oblivious to everything around him. He still looked bored, but in a content, accepting way, as if he didn't really mind that much and was happy just standing there keeping the beat with the music in his head.

I stared at him, for a second wishing I could do it. Wishing I were a little more like Britt. What would be the harm in going over and saying hi?

And then what? my brain demanded in a panic, pinging away more furiously than ever. *You say hi, he says, "Do I know you?" You mumble something about the band. He stares at you like you have two heads. Then his girlfriend comes over and demands to know who you are and what you're doing. You melt into a puddle of humiliation on the floor. . . .*

"I—I can't," I stammered. Ms. Worst-Case Scenario strikes again. "I—I wouldn't know what to say. I—"

At that moment a bunch of students poured out of a nearby doorway, completely blocking my view of Mr. Cute Maybe-Musician. By the time the crowd cleared, there was no sign of him.

I couldn't help feeling a rush of both relief and disappointment. What *was* that?

"I can't believe you chickened out." Britt glared at me in disapproval, pursing her freshly-slicked lips. "He was just your type! I mean, how many guys could actually appreciate that wacked-out band like you do?"

"Yeah, good point," I agreed weakly. "MTIAB isn't for everyone."

"He was probably your soul mate," Britt said. "And now you'll never know. Why don't you ever listen to me?"

There was more, but I wasn't really listening. I knew it all by heart anyway. Plus, my mind was taken up by more important matters. Like figuring out why in the world I'd reacted that way to some random guy I'd never seen before in my life.

Maybe Britt was rubbing off on me at last. Because for the next hour or two I kept catching myself looking for that guy. Every time we gathered for a lecture with one of the other schools; every time we headed back out into the main part of the museum. But there was no sign of him.

"What are you doing?" Britt asked as we stepped into the museum's food-court-style restaurant. We had a half-hour break before the final two events of the day, another lecture and then some kind of planetarium show. Britt and I had decided to revive ourselves with a little caffeine and sugar.

I realized I was doing it again. Scanning

the faces of everyone in the restaurant, looking for that guy.

"Um, I'm just looking for, um, Kris and Vivi?" I blurted out guiltily. "I figured if they're here, we could sit with them."

Britt narrowed her eyes, peering into my face. "No way," she said. "I can't believe it!"

"Can't believe what? That Kris would eat anywhere that wasn't one hundred percent organic-certified?" I joked weakly.

"No. That you're actually still thinking about that guy!" She threw her arms around me, bringing surprised looks from everyone within a twenty yard radius. "My baby's finally growing up!"

"No, I'm not. You're crazy." I yanked away from her. Then I sighed. I can't lie to Britt. She always sees through me. "Okay, so what if I am still thinking about him? I just want to ask him where he got that shirt."

She looked delighted. "See? That's your perfect opening line!" she exclaimed, grabbing my arm and shaking it so hard I almost dropped my purse. "I mean, okay, it's maybe not what *I'd* say, but this is *you* we're talking about. You'll probably do great with that straightforward, nice-girl stuff."

We had to stop talking then as we placed our food orders. I just got a soda. Britt ordered fries as well. When we picked them up, they looked pale and greasy.

"Ew. How can you eat that junk?" I asked.

She popped one of the fries in her mouth as we stepped out into the dining area. "We can't all be raised on some crazy international smorgasbord like—"

"Hey! It's beautiful Britt from Potomac Punk!" a voice yelled, interrupting her.

It was one of Britt's new true loves. Not Trent the Greenleaf Guy; this was one she'd met earlier in the day. He was a little scary— tall and skinny with spiky blond hair, several eyebrow piercings, and a crazy look in his ice-blue eyes. But Britt just thought all that made him look extra hot, like one of the nutty guys from an MTV reality show. She has wide-ranging and sometimes exotic tastes in men, if not in food.

"Tommo!" Britt called back, waving a French fry at him. "Come on, let's go sit with them," she said to me.

We wound our way toward where Tommo was sitting with some friends from his own school, Grove High. By the time we got there, he'd already dragged an extra chair over for Britt. When he saw me coming behind her, he blinked.

"Oh," he said. "Uh, it's Linda, right?"

"Lauren," I corrected. I was used to that. When you travel in Britt's orbit, you get used to being nothing more than a boring, somewhat obsolete little satellite. See? At least I'd picked up some lingo during this trip!

"Okay," Tommo mumbled, glancing around for another free chair. There wasn't one anywhere nearby—the place was pretty crowded, mostly with other high schoolers from our huge group. So Tommo stepped over to some skinny kid with glasses at the next table and poked him on the shoulder. "Bro," he said. "You're almost done, right?"

The kid took one look at him and jumped to his feet. "Um, okay?" he said. Gathering up his half-eaten food, he quickly scooted out of the way as Tommo swung the chair up over his head and set it down in front of me with a flourish.

"There you go, sweetheart," he said, his ice-blue eyes with the undercurrent of crazy meeting mine for a split second before skittering away. He straddled his own chair beside Britt's and leaned closer to her. "So did ya miss me?"

We spent the next few minutes listening to Tommo and his friends show off for Britt. Well, at least Britt was probably listening. I was focusing on my soda and also doing my best to scan the room for a certain guy in a certain T-shirt. Not that I cared that much. I was just curious to see whether that whole pinging thing would happen again if I did see him. Call it scientific curiosity.

I hadn't spotted him by the time an announcement came on in the restaurant ordering Potomac Point and East Elm students back to the atrium for our final seminar of the day. Britt and I stood up.

"Don't go!" Tommo wailed, grabbing her by the arm and pulling her into his lap. "Just blow it off. What are they gonna do?"

Britt giggled, pushing herself back to her feet. "We have to go. Lauren loves all this science stuff—right, babe?"

"Yeah, right," I muttered. "Come on, let's book."

"At least say you'll come to that party next weekend," Tommo said, still not letting go of Britt's arm.

Britt shrugged. "I'll text and let you

know," she said, finally yanking free of him. "Or maybe message you on Facebook. Don't forget to friend me back!"

With that we hurried out of the restaurant, joining the stream of our fellow Potomac Pointers flowing back into the main hall. A few minutes later we were all crowded into a smaller room off the back. A teacher from one of the other schools was in charge of us this time. She was a drill-sergeant type with short, no-nonsense hair but a surprisingly fashion-forward belted dress and Gucci glasses.

"Girls with long hair, please tie it back for safety around the machinery," she told us crisply, her sharp gray eyes darting around to pick out those of us with hair falling past our earlobes.

A kid from my English class named Jared raised his hand. "Dude, what about *guys* with long hair?" he called out, running his other hand through his greasy, dark blond locks.

There were a few snickers. The teacher peered at him over the tops of her glasses. "Guys with long hair should tie it back too," she said. "When you're all ready, we'll proceed. . . ."

I reached into my purse for a rubber band. Working quickly, I pulled my thick hair back, twisting it into a bun with a practiced hand. When you have as much hair as I do, you learn how to keep it under control with a minimum of fuss. It's a vital skill for those embarrassing high-frizz days.

The teacher went on to explain that we would all be sitting in some kind of cockpit and learning about all the doodads inside. We were supposed to pair up and wait our turns.

Britt and I took our place in line. We found ourselves standing behind some couple we didn't know who immediately started making out, complete with loud and fairly disgusting slurping noises, and in front of a pair of exchange students who were chattering to each other in Russian.

"So what do you think of Tommo?" Britt asked. "Think we should hit up that party next weekend?"

"I don't know. He seems kind of cracked out, even for you."

"I know." She giggled. "Isn't he cool? Hey, maybe if we can track down that dream man of yours—"

"You mean the guy with the T-shirt?

I wouldn't call him my dream man. I just thought it was cool that he likes the Beast, that's all."

"Whatever. If we can find him, maybe you can invite him to that party. Wouldn't that be a great opening line?"

"For you, maybe," I said. "But can you really picture me pulling it off? Besides, I'm starting to think maybe he wasn't even with our group. He might've just been some random tourist who stopped in here to use the bathroom or something."

Britt looked alarmed. "I hope not," she said. "You said you never get sparks, but you totally did with him—admit it!"

"I just thought he was cute. Since when is that an admission of true love, let alone this mythical love at first sight? I mean, let's be realistic here—"

"Oh, please." Britt rolled her eyes so hard I was afraid they were going to pop out of her head, like my neighbor's pug dog's had once when I was a kid. "That's so like you. You totally use being a realist to keep from being real."

"That's deep. Did you read it in a fortune cookie?"

"You know I hate Chinese food." Britt

swung her purse, almost hitting the madly Frenching couple. "But stop changing the subject. I just want to know one thing. If we do see that guy again, are you going to do anything about it?"

I stopped to think about that. As soon as I pictured him, my brain started pinging again. Uh-oh.

"Let's worry about that if it happens," I said firmly. "But listen, back to this party . . ."

Our cockpit experience was just finishing up when we got the announcement to head into the planetarium for our big finale. The day was almost over. Finally.

All the schools were coming together for this show, which meant the place was packed. Britt and I filed in and looked around for seats. We saw a group of our friends goofing around near the back, but just as we headed that way, some kids from another school hurried over and took all the remaining seats in their row.

"Come on." Britt grabbed my hand and dragged me toward the front. "There are some spots up here."

"If we can't find seats, maybe we'll have to head back to the bus early," I said hopefully.

But Britt was making a beeline for the seats she'd spotted. We snagged the last two in the middle of the second row. A few other people hadn't found a spot yet and were milling around up near the edge of the room. I glanced at them, mostly just checking to see if any of our friends were up there.

Then I froze. I didn't see any of my friends. But I did see someone else I recognized.

"It's him!" I blurted out before I could stop myself.

Britt had been digging around in her purse, probably planning to check BBB for new messages now that she was safely out of teacher view. But at my words she sat up straight and spun around like some kind of boy-seeking missile.

"Who? You mean *him* him?" she hissed eagerly. Following my gaze, she spotted him too and let out a gasp. "OMG, it *is* him! You've got to go over there, Lauren!"

"What? No! Are you kidding?" I was feeling flustered. Even though I'd been looking for the guy in the MTIAB T-shirt all afternoon, I guess I'd sort of given up on actually finding him. Maybe even started to assume that he was some kind of mirage brought on by too much boredom.

But now here he was again, just a dozen yards away from where I was sitting. He was talking to a couple of other guys, chatting with them and laughing at whatever they were saying. He looked even cuter when he smiled; it lit up his whole face and made him look so friendly and interesting that I could hardly stand it.

As I watched, the other guys bumped fists with The Guy and then wandered away. That left him standing there by himself. He leaned back against the wall, one hand shoved into the pocket of his jeans, not seeming in any particular hurry to find a seat. I couldn't help admiring his cool. If it had been me standing there all alone, I would have felt totally self-conscious. But it didn't seem to bother him at all.

"What are you waiting for?" Britt gave me a shove. "Hurry—the show's going to start soon!"

I hesitated. Once again I found myself wishing for some of Britt's natural confidence. Maybe then I'd be able to take advantage of the second chance that had just fallen into my lap. . . .

Beside me Britt was practically vibrating with impatience. "Are you going to do it, or do I have to go play matchmaker for you?" she demanded. "Because I'll totally do it!" She brightened. "Actually, maybe it's not such a bad idea. I mean, you *are* new to this. What could I say, though? I guess I could go with the truth—just walk over and say, 'Hey, my friend over there thinks you're sexy, but she's too shy to tell you.'" She considered that for a split second, then shook her head. "Nah, too boring. Maybe I could pretend it was all my idea to set you two up because of the band thing. Or I know—I could just invite him to sit over here, since it looks like he doesn't have a seat, and then just casually mention that you happen to be single—"

"No thank you!" I cut her off before she could go on. "If I want to be totally humiliated, I can do it myself."

"So do it then." She gave me another little push. "Hurry! This could be your last chance."

I shot the guy another look. Still standing there. Still looking cool. Too cool for me?

For a second I was ready to chicken out as usual. After all, what were the odds that things would work out even if I did go over there? How likely was it that I wouldn't trip over my tongue, he wouldn't think I was pushy for coming over, it wouldn't turn out that he'd borrowed that T-shirt from a friend and we actually had nothing in common . . . ?

I was ready to let it go, to give up. But as I stared at him, I felt that weird pinging sensation start up again. Sparks?

"Go on," Britt urged. "Take a chance, for once."

That was all it was, I reminded myself. Taking a chance. Giving it a try. If it didn't work and I ended up embarrassed? Britt was right. I'd never have to see the guy again. And if it *did* work? Well, I wasn't sure. But maybe it was worth finding out?

"Okay," I blurted out before I could overthink it any more. "I guess I will go over and say hi."

I stood up, ignoring both Britt's shocked and delighted expression and my own rising panic. Now all I had to do was get over there, which wasn't going to be quite as easy as it sounds. The seats on either side of us were all filled. I decided to scoot out the left side of the row, even though the guy was off to the right. There were only a few seats to the left and like a dozen or more the other way.

I climbed over Britt, then the blond girl sitting next to her. Blondie shot me an annoyed look as I stepped on her foot.

"Excuse me," I mumbled. I kept my gaze focused on the girl in the next seat, hoping to get past without maiming her, too. "I just need to—"

At that moment the lights cut out. The place was pitch-black. Hoots and hollers and giggles rose from all around the planetarium. I could only imagine the groping and pinching and related mischief that had to be going on under the cover of the sudden darkness.

I froze as an announcement came on that the show was about to start. Something about the Big Bang and the birth of the universe. Now what was I supposed to do?

It was tempting to take this as a sign to give up. But when the girl I was standing over gave me a shove and muttered something impatient under her breath, I shook off the feeling. It was too late to turn back now.

I kept going, pushing past the second girl's legs. How many more seats were left in the row? One? Two? I couldn't quite remember. Being in the dark that way was totally disorienting, sort of like swimming with your eyes closed.

"Excuse me," I whispered, feeling around for the next seat back. Instead I felt my hand close over an arm. A thick, hairy arm.

"Hey, honey," a male voice said. "Looking for a seat? There's one right here on my lap."

Ew! I shook off his pawing hands, shoving my way past him as quickly as I could manage. Grabbing for the next seat, I almost did a nosedive as I hit only empty air. Whew! I was out of the row.

Now all I had to do was find my way around the front to that guy. There were tiny running lights marking the aisles, but they weren't much help with anything more than an inch off the floor. So I just turned and walked blindly in the direction I'd last seen Mr. T-shirt. I wasn't quite sure what I was going to do when I got there. Maybe just cling to the wall and wait for the end of the show to approach him.

I walked on as carefully as I could in what I hoped was the right direction. One foot in front of the other . . .

A sudden explosion of sound and light caught me by surprise. It was as if the entire roof of the planetarium had just blown off in some huge explosion. I gasped and leaped forward in a panic. My foot caught an uneven spot on the floor and I tripped, flying forward.

"Oof!"

I felt myself hit something. Or rather some*one*. A pair of strong arms caught me just in time to stop me from hurtling us both right into the wall.

"Sorry!" I gasped, looking up just as another burst of light went off overhead.

My eyes widened. Standing there, his face only inches from mine, was The Guy!

Three

The lights dimmed again. I was sure my face was bright red, and for a second I was afraid I might faint or hurl or something equally embarrassing, just like one of my sick little worst-case-scenario fantasies.

Instead I blurted out the first thing that popped into my head: "We should really stop meeting like this."

The guy laughed. "I don't know about that," he said. "Have we met before? Because somehow I feel really, um, *close* to you right now."

I giggled self-consciously, doing my best to disentangle myself from him. He helped me as best as he could in the near dark, steadying me by holding on to my arms as I struggled to find my balance.

Up on the planetarium's huge, rounded ceiling screen, the Big Bang seemed to be over. The only light came from a sprinkling of stars up there and those little running lights along the floor, making it hard to see much of anything in between. Pretty much all I could make out of the guy was his outline. But he wasn't letting up on his grip on my arms, and I could tell he was peering at me, trying to get a better look at my face.

Feeling strangely bold in the dark, I tried to channel Britt by tossing my hair around a little. I figured that should look pretty sexy even in silhouette. Everyone always said my hair was my best feature, right?

It wasn't until I felt nothing but the soft thump-thump of my bun on the back of my head that I remembered. I still had my hair pulled back from the earlier cockpit thing. Oh well.

But hair or no hair, I could tell that this was definitely what Britt would call a Moment. The guy's grip tightened on my arms, and he leaned a little closer. I could smell coffee and soap and some faint, spicy scent that I guessed was his aftershave.

We were way beyond pinging by now; I

could feel the sparks flying between me and this guy I'd never met before, so strong that for one crazy moment I thought I might grab him by the face and kiss him. It was such an intense urge that I suddenly felt weirded out and was afraid I might start laughing or hyperventilating or something.

"The Beast," I said abruptly, pushing back a little until he let me go. "Um, I mean, your T-shirt. I noticed it before. You like the Beast?"

"The Beast is the best!" His voice was enthusiastic. "So you're into them too? That's cool! I don't know many girls who like that kind of music."

"Oh, totally," I replied. "Have you downloaded their new song yet? It rocks."

"I know, right? Probably their best since 'Squid for Breakfast.'"

"'Squid for Breakfast'? That's only my favorite song of theirs ever!" I exclaimed.

"Mine too." I still couldn't see his face. But I was pretty sure from his voice that he was smiling.

I was smiling too. Maybe all it took for me to pick up a guy was a little pitch darkness. Or maybe all I was waiting for was this particular guy. Either way, I had the feeling that for once, maybe I was getting this right.

The guy leaned a little closer again. "So are you going to tell me your name, or—"

A small but intense beam of light suddenly blinked on out of nowhere, shining directly into his face. He squinted, raising one hand to block it. By squinting a little myself, I could make out the stern face of a middle-aged scientist lady in a lab coat and a name tag. The beam was coming from the tiny flashlight she was pointing at us.

"Do you mind?" she snapped, her voice librarian-quiet but just as stern as her face. "This is a planetarium, not Makeout Point. Please take your seats before I have to report you to your chaperones."

"S-sorry," I stammered.

"Wait," the guy said.

"Now!" Stern Scientist Lady barked. She grabbed me by the arm, dragging me off in the direction of the seats.

"So you never got his name?" Britt asked. "Or where he goes to school, or anything?"

"I already told you a million times. No." I slumped in my seat on the bus, playing with the fraying duct tape someone had used to repair the back of the seat ahead of mine. We were on our way back to Potomac Point. In the back of the bus Johnny Munson and his slacker buddies were singing their own creative version of "Ninety-Nine Bottles of Beer on the Wall." I guess Mr. Feldman and the other teachers were pretty tired after the long day in D.C., because they weren't objecting or even paying attention.

The planetarium show had seemed to go on forever. I'd spent it hunched in the front-row seat where Stern Scientist Lady had stuck me. True to form, Britt had leaped immediately to the best-case scenario when I hadn't returned, and had happily distracted herself throughout the birth and toddler years of the universe or whatever by imagining that Mr. Hottie McHot and I were tucked away somewhere making out or swearing our eternal love or at least getting to know each other better. So when I'd caught up with her during the mass exit looking bored and grumpy, she hadn't been willing to believe it at first. Hence her asking me umpty-bajillion times what had happened.

"Now I wish the trip had lasted longer," she said, idly scrolling through her messages on BBB. "Maybe we could've tracked him down again. Or maybe he would've tracked *you* down. It sounds like he was kind of digging you until Doctor Killjoy came along."

"Yeah. Except he doesn't know my name either. Or even what I look like. Anyway, I tried to look for him afterward, but I'm lucky I even found *you* in that crowd." I sighed, thinking back to my brief but incredible encounter with Mr. Amazing. "You know, I think I finally figured out what you meant by sparks, too. I still don't really *get* it, especially since he couldn't even go by looks since he couldn't really, you know, *see* me—"

"Love at first sight isn't that literal. It's not just about looks. It's, like, pheromones and stuff, too." She beamed at me. "Anyway, don't worry, babe. We may not know who he is, but we know he goes to school somewhere in the county. We can track him down if we put our minds to it."

I couldn't help feeling dubious. "There were nine schools on this trip," I reminded her. "How are we going to find one random guy out of eight other schools? Keep transferring until we run into him?"

"Not necessary." She waved BBB at

me. "I know guys at almost all those other schools. I can ask around."

"And say what? That your spastic loser friend can't even pick up a guy without screwing it up?"

Okay. So I wasn't in the best mood. A day of staring at spaceships topped off by getting accused of groping a guy by the Hall Monitor from Hell can do that to a girl. Or at least to me.

Britt threw her arm around me and gave me a sympathetic squeeze. "I know how you feel, babe."

"Doubtful," I muttered. "When's the last time you actually cared what some guy thought of you?"

That's one of the great things about Britt. She knows when I'm venting and never takes it personally.

"Just leave it to me, okay?" she said. "I'll track this guy down if it's the last thing I do."

That was sweet. But maybe a little ominous, knowing Britt. I shot her a suspicious look.

"I'm not sure that's a good idea," I said. "We don't really have much to go on. What if you end up 'finding' the wrong guy? That could be even more embarrassing than my little falling-into-his-arms trick." I shuddered anew at the memory, though I had to admit it hadn't turned out too badly.

"Do you think I'm an amateur?" Britt grinned. "Besides, how many guys would admit to liking that beastly band?"

"Hey! The Beast rules," I retorted automatically. But my mind was turning all this over. Maybe all hope wasn't lost after all. "Do you really think you can figure out who he is?"

"I know I can." Britt is nothing if not confident in all things. "Just give me time and I'll deliver Mr. Sparks."

Sparks. Was that really what that had been? Sparks, pheromones, love at first sight? Was all this angst worth it, or was I deluding myself?

I glanced out the window at the scenery rushing by. We were almost out of the city by now, and the buildings were thinning, the landscape getting greener and more suburban. With Britt sounding so confident, it was hard to argue with her. Still, my worst-case-scenario tendencies were running full strength, inventing all the ways her plans could backfire.

"You won't embarrass me, will you?" I

asked. "If you do find him, you're not going to, like, tell him you think we're soul mates or whatever, are you? Or that I'm madly in love with him or something?"

She looked vaguely guilty, leading me to believe that was exactly what she'd planned to do. "If you don't want me to contact him, I won't," she said. "I'll just find him and leave the rest to you. Pinky swear."

Britt never breaks a pinky swear. So I lifted my pinky and we made it official.

"But that doesn't mean I'm going to let you get away with wussing out on me," she warned. "If I find him for you, you have to promise to do something about it."

"Look, I'll promise to do something," I said. "But I can't promise it'll be what *you* would do. I'm not you, okay?"

She didn't look completely satisfied with that. But she nodded. "Good enough, I guess."

We pinky-swore again on that. Then I took a deep breath, feeling a nervous little flutter run through me like a stampede of ants skittering through my guts.

"Okay," I said. "Go find him. And then we'll just have to see what happens after that."

Four

A couple of days later I sat at the kitchen table stirring my cereal and thinking about the guy in the Beast T-shirt. Britt hadn't found him yet, which was almost a relief. It was still sort of freaking me out, the way I'd reacted to him. As if I knew him already. Or at least as if I knew I *wanted* to know him. Really, really wanted to.

What would make me feel that way? Sure, the guy was cute. No question. But there were lots of good-looking guys in the world, and I'd never reacted to any of them with the instant crazies. So what was it? That T-shirt? Doubtful. Otherwise I'd have been throwing myself, Britt-style, at every guy at the last MTIAB concert I'd attended. No, it just didn't make sense. And that bugged me.

"Mroh-ah-rohwww!"

I blinked as the family cat jumped onto the table in one graceful movement. Deceptively graceful. One paw almost landed in my bowl. It actually did land on my spoon, flipping it off the table.

Meow Tse Tung is a blue-point Siamese. He looks sleek and elegant with his velvety gray-and-cream coat and vibrant sapphire-blue eyes. But in truth he's a nut.

"Morning, Chairman," I said, reaching over to pat him. He bumped his head up into my hand, then started sniffing at the milk in my bowl.

"Get that monster off the table," my mother ordered as she hurried into the room. She was dressed in what she calls her Capitol Hill uniform: a navy blue suit with a conservative straight skirt and a beige blouse, finished off with panty hose, sensible short-heeled navy pumps, and discreet gold jewelry. Every time I try to liven up her look with a little color, more modern shapes and fabrics, or maybe just some more interesting jewelry, she shoots me down. Apparently, people at the Library of Congress, where she works as a research librarian, have no appreciation for fashion.

"Chairman Meow was just saying hi," I said. But I scooped up the cat and deposited him on the floor with a yowl of protest. His yowl, not mine. While I was down there, I retrieved my spoon.

Mom paused to peer at my breakfast on her way to the coffee pot. "What's that you're eating? Cereal? There's still some leftover *nasi lemak* in the fridge, you know."

"I know. It's starting to look kind of gross, especially this early in the morning. Cornflakes are just fine."

I should probably mention that my family is a little weird about food. My parents are really into exploring ethnic cuisines. They try to test out a new one at least two weeks out of every month, with the other weeks featuring what they call "reruns"— returns to favorite cuisines we've tried in the past. This week it was Malaysian food, last week it was Turkish, and next week might find us sampling the unique delicacies of Finland or Sri Lanka or maybe Mars, if my parents could find a cookbook or some recipes on the Internet. Because of this, plain old American cereal was pretty much an exotic treat in our house, and I was lucky if Dad remembered to stop at the regular supermarket to buy stuff like OJ and bread on his way home from shopping at whatever specialty market he was hitting up that week. Britt always brought her own snacks when she came to sleep over.

My mom checked her watch. "Crap," she muttered. "I'm going to miss the train if I don't get out of here."

Just then my dad zoomed in. He zooms everywhere; he has tons of energy, even at the advanced age of forty-four. I guess that's how he survives his job as a middle school social studies teacher over in the next district. He's even more hyper than most of his students.

"Has anyone seen those papers I was grading last night?" he asked breathlessly, doing his best to tie his tie while circling the kitchen like some kind of whirling dervish. "I was supposed to be at school five minutes ago, and I can't find them anywhere!" He paused to cock one eye down at the tie, which looked sort of like a kite tail that had been caught in a windmill. "Dang it! Lauren, why'd I ever let you convince me to start wearing these things?"

"Because clip-on ties should be banished from polite society." I stepped over and pushed his hands away. "Here, I'll do it."

Within seconds I had the tie—a supercool Sovereign Beck I'd given him for his last birthday—properly tied and looking jaunty with the shirt I'd also picked out for him. If only he'd let me talk him into shaving off his messy sideburns, neatening his beetle brows, and touching up his gray, he'd actually be looking pretty swank.

"Did you check on top of the breakfront?" Mom asked him. "I think I remember you sticking them up there to keep them away from the cat."

His eyes lit up. "You're a genius, Liz!" he cried. Pausing just long enough to plant a lip-smacking kiss on her forehead, he zipped out of the room.

Mom chuckled as she wiped Dad's drool off her face. For some reason that brought me back to my earlier train of thought.

"Hey, Mom," I said. "I know you and Dad met in college. But how long was it before you knew he was the one?"

"The one what?" Mom had turned away to pour coffee into a commuter cup. She sounded kind of preoccupied.

"The One," I said again. "You know. The one for you. The guy you wanted to spend the rest of your life with."

She capped her cup and shot me a surprised look. No wonder. It wasn't the kind of question I normally asked over breakfast. Or anytime, really.

"Oh, I don't know," she said with a chuckle. "I guess it was when he got my car running again when it broke down right before an important internship interview."

"Got them!" Dad raced back in waving a messy sheaf of papers over his head.

"Good." Mom checked her watch, then grabbed her coffee cup. "I'm out of here. Lauren, maybe your father can give you a more thorough answer to your question."

"What question?" Dad asked as Mom gave him a peck on the cheek and rushed out the back door.

"I was just asking how you two knew you were meant for each other," I said. "Romantically, I mean. How soon after you met, that kind of thing."

"I think she fell for me the first time I fixed that beater car of hers." Dad guffawed at his own joke as I rolled my eyes. However they'd met, the two of them were a match made in heaven, that was for sure. At least when it came to their lame sense of humor.

Soon Dad hurried off to work too, leaving me alone in the kitchen. Well, not quite alone. I turned back to my cereal to find Meow Tse Tung purring blissfully as he lapped the last of the milk out of my bowl.

When I got to school, Britt was waiting for me at my locker. "I found him!" she shrieked as soon as she saw me coming. She raced toward me, waving BBB over her head. "OMG, I totally found him! I told you I'd do it! It took me a little longer than I thought, but hey, I'm not a miracle worker or anything."

I blinked. "Found who? Oh!" My morning fog cleared instantly as I caught on. Yeah, I'm a little slow before nine a.m. "Wait. Really?"

"I've been scouring Facebook all week, focusing on people from the schools that were on the trip," Britt explained. "I figured your mystery guy would turn up on somebody's feed sooner or later. And I'm pretty sure I finally figured out who he might be!"

"Might?" My mind was churning. I wasn't sure what to think.

She looked proud of herself. "I told you I'd be careful and not embarrass you, right? So instead of following up, I figured I'd let you check it out for yourself. I actually found him on that guy Tommo's wall—turns out they go to the same school. Here, see for yourself. His name's Riley."

"Riley," I murmured, nodding. The name fit him. Riley.

I took BBB and looked at her tiny screen. Britt had it open to her Facebook wall.

"Tommo reposted an entry from his wall," Britt explained. "Riley's, I mean. Trying to help spread the word, I guess."

"Spread the word?" I stared at her, suddenly suspicious. "Wait, you didn't tell that Tommo guy about me or—"

"No, chill out! That's not what I mean. Here." She grabbed BBB back and scrolled down a bit.

Then she handed the BlackBerry back to me, pointing. I gasped.

"That's him!" I exclaimed when I saw the profile photo beside the entry she'd indicated.

Pinging was happening all over the

place. The photo was miniscule, but that didn't matter. I recognized him instantly. Riley. The guy from the planetarium.

"Read what he wrote!" Britt was jigging and twitching like a monkey on speed.

It was a challenge to tear my gaze away from that picture to look at the text beside it. I could hardly believe Britt had actually found him.

"'Searching for a certain girl,'" I read aloud. "'I met you in the planetarium during the class trip this week and can't stop thinking about you. But I never got your name, your school, or even a good look at you . . .'"

There was more, but I had to stop for a second to process this. I stared at Britt, blinking rapidly.

"Wait," I said. "He's talking about *me*, right?"

"Right!" She started jumping up and down in earnest now. Unable to control her glee, she flung her arms around me and we both started dancing around right there in the crowded school hallway. Missy McManus, the most annoying teacher's pet in the entire school, gave us a disapproving look as she swished past. Chaz Markus paused just long enough to whistle and call out something crude about Britt's anatomy. Everyone else ignored us. The entire school is pretty much used to Britt's exuberance.

My heart was pounding and my throat was dry. I felt excited, nervous, and weirded out all at the same time. This was big. Huge, in fact. I wasn't sure I was ready to handle it.

Finally we stopped dancing. Then I read the rest of the entry:

Searching for a certain girl: I met you in the planetarium during the class trip this week and can't stop thinking about you. But I never got your name, your school, or even a good look at you. You fell into my arms and told me that we've got to stop meeting like this, but I can't stop thinking about how we met. I keep humming the song I wrote about you, and it's driving my friends crazy. So if you're The One, and you want to talk about the Beast and have some of your favorite squid for breakfast, please get in touch . . . and maybe we can stop meeting like that, and meet for real.

"Wow," I said, stunned. "He wrote a song. About meeting me."

"Isn't that super amazingly awesome and cool?" Britt exclaimed, clutching my arm so hard it hurt. "This has got to be the most romantic thing that's ever happened in real life!"

I wanted to respond to that, to tease her about putting my love life ahead of her many conquests. But I couldn't focus on that.

"I have to write back," I said. "I should friend him and, you know, write something. I guess."

The very idea was daunting. Luckily, I was saved by the bell. Literally. The late bell jangled overhead, reminding me that I was supposed to be in homeroom.

"Oops." Britt grabbed BBB back and stuffed her in her bag. "Let's pick this up later. If I'm late to homeroom one more time this year, Old Lady Watson is going to expel me."

"What are you typing? Come on, let me see!" Britt said.

"I don't know. Everything I write sounds so lame." I hit the delete button, then glanced over my shoulder at Britt. She was sitting on the edge of my bed, tickling Chairman Meow, who was sprawled out on his back beside her, purring like a maniac.

I'd had a yearbook meeting during lunch that day, and Britt and I didn't have the same study hall. So we'd decided to head to my house after school so she could be there for moral support while I wrote to Riley.

Unfortunately, once I'd sat down at my desk in front of my laptop, found Riley again, and clicked on Add as Friend, I'd realized I had no idea what to say to him. The little Add a Personal Message box blinked impatiently at me, once again as blank as the proverbial slate.

"What?" Britt blinked impatiently at me too. "Why aren't you typing? The sooner you write back, the sooner you get to start your fabulous new romance with Mr. Cutie Pie." She tickled Meow under the chin, which made him yawn and stretch.

"I just don't know what to say that doesn't make me sound like a total dork." I sighed, closing my eyes to avoid that taunting blank box. "Nothing I try seems right."

"How about this: 'Meeting you was out of this world' . . ." She paused and grinned, waggling her eyebrows like Groucho Marx. "Get it? You know, because you met at the planetarium? Cute, huh?"

I rolled my eyes. "Get real. I thought you were supposed to be good at this."

"Okay, okay, give me a minute. I'm just getting warmed up." She tapped her chin thoughtfully with one manicured finger. "How about, 'Greetings from The One. Are you The One for me? Let's see if One and One make Two of a Kind.'"

"Are you kidding me?" I shook my head. "So totally not me."

She frowned. "Come on, you've got to write something! Oh! I know." She sat up so fast she startled Meow, who leaped to his feet and dashed away, almost bonking himself into the wall as he jumped down off the bed. "How about, 'Roses are red, violets are blue; I'll be your One, if you'll be my Two.'"

"That doesn't even make sense."

"Maybe not. But it's cute and catchy and sort of romantic." Britt pursed her lips. "Well, actually, now that you mention it, maybe it's a little corny."

"A little?"

"Okay, a lot." She giggled. "But guys eat that kind of crap up."

I wrinkled my nose. "Maybe when *you* say it," I said. "Especially if you happen to be fluttering your eyelashes and giving them that *hello, big boy* look of yours at the same time." I shook my head, glancing back at the blinking cursor on the screen. "Anyway. I think we may be trying too hard here. I'm just trying to let this guy know I'm out here, not wow him with my mad poetry skillz."

"It doesn't have to be poetry," Britt said. "Just something fun and clever to catch his attention."

I didn't answer, instead quickly typing a few lines: *Hi there! I'm the girl from the planetarium. My name is Lauren, and I thought you seemed really cool, too. Write back if you want to chat more.*

"There," I said, sitting back from the keyboard and shooting Britt a look that dared her to argue that my note was too boring and straightforward. "That should do the trick."

"Are you sure?" To her credit, Britt didn't say anything else as she scanned the lines. But she definitely looked dubious.

I took a deep breath, nodded, then hit the Send Request button. "Why play games?" I said, feeling a shiver of nervousness as I saw the message blink away into cyberspace. "If those sparks—or whatever they were—really were some kind of hint that this guy and I are right for each other, he should be fine with the real me. If not, then oh well."

Britt shrugged. "I guess you're right. Come on, I'll give you a mani-pedi while you wait to hear back from him. Your nails look like hell."

"No they don't." I held out my hands to check. "Hmm. Okay, maybe they do."

Britt rolled over and grabbed a bottle of pink polish off my bedside table. "You'll want to look your best when you meet Mr. Right."

It was only a few minutes before my e-mail beeped to let me know I had a new message. I jumped a little at the sound. So did Chairman Meow. He'd returned to his spot on the bed by now, but the tiny little beep sent him bolting back under the bed. Crazy cat.

"What's with him?" Britt said, staring after him.

I didn't respond. I'd just clicked over to my inbox, carefully avoiding getting wet polish on the keyboard. My heart jumped when I saw that the new message was from Facebook. Riley had accepted my friend request.

"Click through!" Britt ordered, leaning so close that she was practically resting her chin on my shoulder. "See what he says!"

I obeyed, clicking on the message link. It opened immediately, filling the screen. Mostly with blank space.

Hi Lauren, Riley had written. *Nice to hear from you.*

That was all. No proclamations of love at first sight. Not even a proclamation of like, lust, or vague interest. Just hi-how-ya-doing. It wasn't quite what I'd expected after that sweet, romantic "searching" post.

"Wow," I said. "He doesn't exactly sound thrilled and overjoyed to hear from The One, does he?"

"So what? Your thing was short and boring too. Just click through!" Britt bounced up and down on the edge of my bed. "OMG, this is so exciting! I can't wait to see what's on his page."

I shrugged. She had a point. Maybe Riley and I had more in common than our taste for MTIAB. Like not knowing what to type to a perfect stranger on a social networking site.

Reaching for the mouse, I clicked on the link to take me to Riley's profile page. It popped up on the screen.

The first thing I saw was his profile picture. He looked even better full-size than he had on Britt's BlackBerry. The photo showed him standing with a bicycle on a wooded trail somewhere, a grin on his face and the wind blowing his hair around. Nice.

Next I turned to the text, scanning down the latest posts. And suddenly I started to understand why he hadn't sounded more excited to hear from me. Because his wall was positively flooded with messages from girls who'd read his "searching" post.

And almost every single one of them was claiming to be The One!

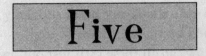

Five

"I can't believe this!" I exclaimed, outraged. I scrolled down the page. Farther and farther. There had to be dozens of entries on there from all different girls. I scanned a few:

Hi Riley! I'm The One ur looking 4. Would luv to c u again!

Riley: When I said we should stop meeting like this, I already knew we were 2 of a kind. Would luv to meet u again — and show u how much I liked meeting u. BB4N!

**Hi again cutie! Would love 2 get 2gether &
hear the song u wrote after we met. Luv, yr
Planetarium Girl xoxo**

There were plenty more along the same
lines. I just shook my head, suddenly overwhelmed by the weirdness of it all.

"How can all these girls just out-and-out
lie like that?" I wondered aloud. "Especially
to such a cool guy who, like, laid his heart
out there so honestly and everything?"

"That's sort of the point, I guess." Britt
was reading along over my shoulder. "Who
wouldn't jump at the chance to snag such
an amazingly romantic guy? Hey, if I saw
his message and didn't know you were The
One, I might've tried responding myself."
She grinned weakly as I shot her an evil
look.

"Well, *I'd* never do anything like that."
I turned my glare back to the screen, feeling
annoyed. "Maybe I should just forget this
whole thing. I hate playing games."

"What?" Britt looked alarmed. "Babe,
you can't give up now. Not when you just
found him!"

"Yeah, me and the entire female popula-
tion of southern Maryland," I said sourly.

Britt was scanning the entries again. Suddenly she gasped. "Check it out! Some chick used my idea to say meeting him was out of this world." When she realized I was glaring at her again, she sat back. "But that's not important right now. What *is* important is for you to let him know that you really *are* his planetarium girl."

"Why bother?" I slumped in my chair, feeling cranky. "If he doesn't realize it's me on his own, maybe this wasn't meant to be after all."

"Sure it was. Come on, you can't give up now! Seriously." Britt crouched down and grabbed me by the knees, staring up into my face with a totally sincere expression. "Look, Lauren. I've never seen you react to someone like this before. That has to mean something, right? Isn't this guy worth at least a little more effort?"

My gaze wandered back to Riley's profile pic. I shrugged.

"You *know* I'm right," Britt said. "I mean, what if this Riley guy is the love of your life, and you just sit back and let some other Facebook hussy grab him?"

"Love of my life? Let's not get carried away here." But I had to admit she had a point, maybe. Was it too soon to give up? "I guess he admitted himself that he doesn't really know what I look like," I said slowly. "So how would he know it's really me and not just another faker?"

"That's the spirit!" Britt bounced to her feet, grinning like a fool. "All you have to do is be your gorgeous, witty self and he'll figure it out."

"Maybe you're right."

I still felt kind of irritated at all those deceptive girls out there in FB Land. But my moment of hopelessness had passed, at least mostly. Maybe Britt was right. Maybe it was worth at least trying to show Riley who I really was. What was the worst that could happen? At least it was a little easier to be brave over the Internet than in real life.

I took a deep breath. "I guess I could write him back and see where things go from there."

"Definitely!" Britt exclaimed, looking as thrilled as if she'd just won the lottery and landed a date with Orlando Bloom at the same time. It doesn't take much to make her happy. "So what are you going to say?"

"I don't know." But my fingers were

already reaching for the keys. I clicked on the Send Riley a Message link beneath his photo.

This time the words came pretty easily, and I just let them flow, trying not to overthink things too much. When I finished, I sat back and read over what I'd just typed:

Hi Riley, thanks for friending me back. Meeting at the planetarium like that was crazy, huh? But mostly I'm just psyched to find someone else who appreciates MTIAB like I do. Did u see the latest update on their blog? Funny pix from their last show down in VA.

I sent the message. "There," I said. "Maybe that'll make him realize it's really me. I bet all those other girls have never even heard of the Beast."

"Yeah," Britt said dubiously. "Unless they actually, you know, read Riley's info page. There's stuff about that crazy band all over it, including a link to their site and a bunch of downloads. Guess he's really into them. But then again, nobody's perfect."

Glancing back at her, I saw that she had BBB out. She was lounging on my bed, scrolling away, having clearly logged onto FB using my password. I guess that's what I get for giving it to her. Chairman Meow, who had reappeared once again, was sitting there watching her intently, probably wondering if BBB was some kind of exotic mouse that he should attack and wrestle away from her. For his sake I hoped he didn't try it. Britt would fight a cougar to keep BBB safe, let alone a spoiled Siamese.

"Oh," I mumbled, as what Britt was saying sunk in. "Guess I never thought of that."

At first I felt kind of stupid. Of course. Any girl who was willing to lie like a rug about being Planetarium Girl was probably willing to put in a little research effort to make her story sound good. In fact, when I clicked back to Riley's profile page and scrolled down a little farther, I saw that Britt was right. Several of the earlier responders had mentioned MTIAB somewhere in their posts. And when I got back to the first few alleged Planetarium Girls—the ones Riley had actually replied back to a few times—I saw that there had been a few conversations about the band. Including at least two who claimed that "Squid for Breakfast" was, like, their favorite song ever in the history of the universe.

My heart sank. It seemed it might not be easy proving I was the real deal after all.

But I quickly shrugged that off. "It doesn't matter," I told Britt. "He'll realize soon enough that I'm a real fan and not a poser. The main thing is getting to know him, and him getting to know me. That's the only way we'll be able to tell if we're right for each other."

"You already know that." Britt glanced up from BBB and waggled her eyebrows. "Love at first sight, remember? Pheromones never lie."

"Whatever." I turned back to the screen as I heard a blip. Riley had just written back!

Hi Lauren! Saw those pix on the blog. 2 funny!
I can't believe someone squirted Ty w/shaving
cream! So great that he kept it on his head 4
the rest of the show. Those guys r a blast!
So I guess ur really into the band, huh?

I smiled. He sounded a lot friendlier already. Better yet, he sounded every bit as enthusiastic about the Beast as I was. That made him seem even cooler.

Britt stood up and stepped closer to read over my shoulder, leaving BBB defenseless on the bed with Meow. The cat crouched down and stared at the helpless PDA with narrowed blue eyes, his long, slender gray tail twitching. But I barely spared that little drama a glance before turning my attention back to Riley's words.

"Sounds like he's a true fan," I murmured.

"What are you waiting for? He's obviously hanging on your every word. So write back already!" Britt poked me in the arm.

"Ow!" I slapped her finger away. Then I turned back to the keyboard.

Def. way into the Beast. I've been a fan ever since I first heard their demo last year. Been 2 at least 5 shows since then. They r great live! Have u been?

"Aren't you going to talk about anything but that wacked-out band?" Britt complained. "You should try saying something romantic. Maybe tell him how cute he looks in his profile pic. Or remind him how sexy his manly arms felt when he held you at the planetarium."

"Yeah, right." I rolled my eyes. "Because if I want him to get to know the real me, that's exactly what I'd say."

Just then there was a sudden flurry of motion behind us. Also a couple of dramatic growls and a weird little yip. Glancing back, I saw that Meow had just pounced on BBB and was doing his best to wrestle her into submission.

Britt saw, too. "Hey, get off of that, you mangy creature!" she cried.

I laughed as she lunged for Meow. He saw her coming and leaped straight up into the air, all four paws out like Wile E. Coyote falling off a cliff. As soon as he landed, he zoomed off the bed and straight out of the room. I could hear his claws skittering across the hardwood in the hall outside and a few indignant yowls drifting back toward us.

By the time BBB was safely back in Britt's hand and she'd determined that her baby was none the worse for wear, Riley's response was up on my screen.

I've been 2 like 5 Beast shows too. Plus I'm
going 2 see them this Fri. at the Cave Club.
I can't wait!

"Wow," I said. "He's going to see the
Beast this weekend at the Cave? I can't
believe he got tickets to that show! It sold
out before I could get through on the site.
He's so lucky!"

The Cave Club was in Silver Grove,
the same town as Grove High, where both
Riley and Tommo went. It was an all-ages
club that hosted all kinds of local bands. I'd
been there a few times, including once to
see MTIAB. But the place was pretty small,
and tickets were first come, first served. To
my disappointment I'd been totally shut
out this time.

"Mmm-hmm." Britt didn't seem to be
paying much attention. When I glanced at
her, she had a certain look on her face. A
certain thoughtful, rather devilish look.

"Hey," I said. "What are you—"

Before I could finish, she lunged past
me, knocking me away from the keyboard
with an elbow to the shoulder like some
crazed professional wrestler. She bent over
my laptop, her fingers flying over the keys.

All that texting and BBBing had made her a superfast typist. Before I knew it, she'd written back to Riley and pressed send.

"Wait," I protested. "Was that to Riley? He's going to think that was me! What did you just say to him?"

My stomach clenched as several possibilities flitted through my mind. What if she'd written something about how sexy and adorable he looked in his profile photo, or maybe changed the topic back to our planetarium meeting?

But when I peered at what she'd just sent him, I saw that it was even worse:

Cool! I'm going 2 that Cave show, 2. Maybe I'll c u there!

Six

"Oh my God!" I exclaimed, more than a little annoyed. "Why'd you write that? Didn't you just hear me say that show's sold out?"

"Yeah," Britt said, looking pleased with herself. "I heard you."

I shoved her away from the keyboard. "So what's the big idea telling him I'm going?" I scowled at her. "With my luck, he'll show up and actually decide to look for me there, and end up meeting up with some other girl pretending to be me. Again."

"Don't worry. You're going."

I stared at her. She was smiling, though I wasn't sure why. Britt might not be a straight-A student, but she's no idiot. So why couldn't she comprehend a simple English sentence?

"Listen to me," I said, speaking slowly so she couldn't miss my point this time. "The. Show. Is. Sold. Out. Okay? And I. Do. Not. Have. A. Ticket!"

"I heard you the first time." Britt leaned over the computer as it pinged.

I glanced down at it too. It was another message from Riley: *Cool, c u there.*

Great. Now I was stuck. "What were you thinking?" I exclaimed.

"If you'll stop freaking out for half a second, I'll tell you." Britt moved away from the laptop, flopping back onto my bed. "I'm just thinking that all this cyberflirting is nice and all, but you need to meet up with Riley again in person, ASAP. Once he sees you again, those sparks will come back, and then he'll realize you really are Planetarium Girl."

I wrinkled my nose. "You know I'm not about the game playing . . . ," I began dubiously.

"It's not game playing. You're just meeting up again, not pretending to be anything or anyone you're not."

"Wrong. I'm pretending to be a person with a Beast ticket."

71

She waved one hand airily, as if shooing away that minor detail. "That doesn't matter. All we need to do is arrange for you two lovebirds to bump into each other outside the club. The rest will be romantic history!"

"I don't know. Still sounds like game playing to me."

Britt shrugged. "Okay, maybe a little," she said. "But it's too late to back out now. He thinks you're going."

I glanced at the computer screen, where Riley's last message was still blinking back at me. Then I glanced at Britt. Okay, *glared* at Britt.

Because I realized she was right. It was too late to take back what "I" had told him now without looking like a psycho.

"Thanks a lot, Britt," I muttered.

She smiled serenely. "You're welcome."

"So how's this supposed to work again?" I asked Britt with a flutter of nerves.

It was Friday night. I was standing on a lamplit sidewalk in Silver Grove outside the Cave Club, dressed in a MTIAB T-shirt, my favorite skinny jeans, and a pair of Sanuk flats, along with a cool sparkly vintage belt I'd found at a thrift shop. My hair was flowing free in all its glossy glory, and Britt had spent close to an hour making sure my makeup was perfect. I had to admit it—I felt pretty hot.

At least I would have if I wasn't so anxious I was afraid I might puke at any moment. The band was in full swing inside; the fast-paced strains of their song "My Emergency" poured out to fill the otherwise quiet block with raucous energy. I wondered how the people in the apartments over the Laundromat and liquor store on either side of the club ever got any sleep on the weekends.

Britt was there, too. So was her latest boy toy, a kid she'd met at the gym, named Todd. He was just her type: good-looking, a little dumb, and totally into her. He hadn't asked too many questions about why we were chilling outside the club instead of going in. Instead he kept grabbing Britt and slow-dancing with her right there in the street. At the moment she was giggling and halfheartedly pushing his hands away as he kept grabbing for her butt.

But at my question she smacked him away for real, disentangling herself and turning toward me. "I told you, we just wait here until the show lets out," she explained with remarkable patience, considering we'd been through this umpteen times already. "Then we hang out and watch for him, and when you see him, you go introduce yourself and just sort of let him think you were in there all along." She shrugged. "Not that he'll waste too much time wondering about that anyway. Once he sees you, it's going to be Spark City."

I just nodded, too nervous to speak. Now that I was here, faced with the prospect of seeing Riley again very soon, my palms were sweaty and my heart was pounding away like a jackhammer trying to escape from my chest. What was up with that? Since when did I get so nervous around a cute guy?

Sparks, I reminded myself. *This must be what happens when you get sparks.*

"I don't believe in love at first sight," I muttered, talking mostly to myself.

But Boy Toy Todd heard me. "Yo," he said. "Sure you do. Everyone believes in love at first sight." He grabbed Britt around the waist and pulled her toward him, swaying back and forth without paying the least bit of attention to the rhythm of the song that was playing. "Like, the second I saw Britt straddling that stationary bike, all wrapped in spandex and looking hot, I knew I had to get my hands on her."

"That's not love," I informed him, not in the mood to be tactful. "It's lust."

An expression of dull confusion crossed his handsome face. I wasn't sure whether he literally didn't understand what I meant, or if he just wasn't accustomed to having girls argue with him. Either way, I wasn't interested in continuing the vocabulary lesson. The band had just finished their song, and the distinctive opening strains of "Squid for Breakfast" were drifting out into the night air.

Naturally, that reminded me of Riley. "I'm really not sure about this," I told Britt anxiously. "You know I'm not a good liar. And I still say this really feels like game playing to me."

"Look, you don't actually have to lie." Britt smacked at Todd's hands, which were starting to wander again. "You just have to mingle with the crowd when the show lets out and look for Riley. What's the big deal? It's not like we can't hear the whole show from out here."

"True. The Beast is known for being loud." I smiled, glancing toward the club building. The solid brick walls probably weren't *actually* throbbing with the beat of the song, but it sort of seemed like it.

"And it's not like you aren't really a fan of this ridiculous band." Britt rolled her eyes as the traditional audience sing-along chorus of "Squid! Squid! Squid!" rang out from inside.

"True." I smiled, my foot tapping along with each "Squid."

"Besides," Britt said, "it's for a good cause. True love."

Todd started nibbling on her earlobe right about then, which made me give up on talking to her anymore. Besides, I knew she didn't get why I wasn't comfortable with this. After all, she was right in a way. Listening to the show from outside was almost as good as being in there, and I'd certainly seen the Beast enough times in the past to make up the difference. But I still felt uneasy about deceiving Riley. Didn't that make me no better than all those fibbing Facebookers?

I felt like one of those people in the movies who have a devil on one shoulder and an angel on the other when they're making a big decision. Only in my case it was Britt sitting on one shoulder and my own insecurities on the other. And both of them were yowling at me as loudly as Chairman Meow when he's hungry, making it hard to think rationally.

Maybe I should just go, I thought. *This isn't worth it. I can just tell Riley I couldn't make the show after all. . . .*

My thoughts were interrupted by the sudden ear-shattering banging of cymbals and drums from inside—the Beast's traditional farewell. The show was over.

Seconds later people started emerging from the club, talking and laughing loudly as a result of the deafening show. I smiled despite my nerves, knowing the feeling all too well.

Britt had started slow-dancing with Todd again, but now she pulled away and raced over to grab my arm. "Here we go!" she hissed, her eyes dancing with anticipation. "I'll help you spot him, but don't worry, I'll disappear before he sees me. It's better if he thinks you're alone."

"Why? So he thinks I'm a total loser with no friends?"

"Shh! Pay attention. We don't want to miss him."

But five minutes passed and then ten, with more and more people coming out of the club, and there was still no sign of Riley. I was starting to wonder if I'd hallucinated that whole Facebook exchange when Britt finally got impatient.

"He must be hanging out inside," she said, grabbing my hand and dragging me toward the door. "Come on, let's go see."

"Maybe he couldn't come after all," I said as I allowed myself to be dragged. "His parents might have grounded him or something, or maybe he got the flu. . . ."

"Wait, why are we going in this dump?" Todd complained, trailing along after us. "I thought we were going for pizza after we dropped Lauren off."

"Chillax, Todd," Britt tossed over her shoulder. "You'll get your 'za. First we need to get Lauren her man."

I winced; Britt doesn't have the quietest voice in the world. What if Riley walked out just in time to hear her?

But he didn't. Instead we pushed our way past a rowdy group of college kids rushing out the door, and we finally found ourselves inside the club.

The Cave pretty much lives up to its

name; it's little more than one low-ceilinged room with a small stage at the far end and a few tables scattered across the battered floorboards. The lighting is pretty bad, consisting mostly of bare, flickering overhead bulbs, which made it hard to see much as we wandered farther in.

The band was dismantling their equipment on the stage, laughing and trading obscenity-laced insults with some fans who were watching. Maybe a couple dozen other people were clustered here and there throughout the place, either finishing their drinks or chatting with one another about the show.

"Do you see him?" Britt hissed into my ear, scanning the room.

"See who?" Todd asked too loudly from behind us. "Who are we looking for anyway? Just a single guy for Lauren to hook up with?"

"Ew, no!" Britt shot him an annoyed look. "Who do you think she is, anyway?"

I didn't hear Todd's response. That was because I'd just turned and spotted Riley. He was sitting at one of the tables off to one side.

At first my heart did this funny little

series of somersaults as the pinging started again. He was here—there—right in front of me, just ten yards away. Looking adorable in a Beast T-shirt and jeans, with his hair slightly damp with sweat—it was sweltering in the club.

Then I saw who was sitting with him, and my heart landed from its latest somersault with a splat. He was surrounded by at least three cute girls. And as I watched, one of them laughed and then bent down to plant a kiss right on the top of his head.

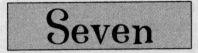

Seven

"Let's get out of here," I hissed at Britt, turning away.

But she'd just spotted Riley, too. "There he is!" she said. "Go for it, babe."

"No way. Looks like he has enough female company already." My hands were shaking, and my stomach churned with disappointment. Coming here had been a mistake. A *huge* mistake. Why had I let Britt talk me into such a crazy plan?

I sneaked another look over at the table. At that same moment Riley looked up—and his eyes locked onto mine. He blinked, then tilted his head and squinted, clearly trying to get a better look in the dim lighting. I flashed back to the field trip; he'd tilted his head the same way while trying to get a look at me in the darkened planetarium.

But this time the lighting wasn't quite *that* bad. If he recognized me from my Facebook profile pic . . .

"Hurry!" I hissed to Britt. "We have to get out of here!"

But when I looked behind me, she'd disappeared. I spun around frantically, finally spotting her halfway across the club, dragging Todd behind her.

I gritted my teeth. Thanks, Britt.

"Hey, Lauren!" a voice called. *Riley's* voice. I would have recognized it anywhere.

I slowly turned around to face him again, plastering a smile on my face. "Oh! Hey," I called back to him. "Uh, there you are."

It was a pretty lame response. But he waved me over anyway.

My feet seemed to take on a life of their own, propelling me toward his table despite the fact that my whole body had just gone numb. I kept my focus on Riley, trying not to notice the three girls, who were now peering at me suspiciously.

When I was still a few feet away, Riley jumped up and took a couple of big strides over to join me. "I've been looking everywhere for you, Lauren," he said, reaching over and giving my arm a friendly squeeze.

I couldn't help staring down at his hand on my arm. "Um . . . ," I said intelligently.

Riley was turning back to the other girls, who were still staring at us from the table. "Listen, it's been nice talking to you," he told them. "But I promised Lauren here that we'd hang out after the show. It's, uh, her birthday today."

"Oh." The girl who'd kissed him on the head, an overdone blonde wearing a low-cut purple cami and too much glitter eye shadow, didn't even bother to hide her disappointment. "Are you sure you have to go so soon?"

"Sorry," Riley said again.

"Happy birthday," one of the other girls said to me with a sickly-sweet fake smile. "So how do you know our Riley?"

"Uh . . . ," I began helplessly.

"Lauren and I are old pals," Riley put in before I could hyperventilate. "Known her forever. Old, old pals. So anyway, bye!"

"Bye, Riley! I'll catch you later on Facebook!" the blonde sang out.

"Me too!" the third girl put in. "I'm still

dying to talk to you about our meeting at the planetarium."

Riley just smiled and nodded, then turned away and pulled me along with him, steering me gently toward the exit. I was so focused on keeping my numb feet and legs from tripping over themselves and sending me flying that I didn't have enough mental energy left over to wonder exactly what was happening. Moments later we burst out into the evening air, which felt cool and refreshing after the stuffy interior of the club.

That revived me a little, restoring at least part of my usual abilities to think and speak. "Who—what—," I stammered.

Okay. I *said* it was partial.

He let go of my arm and turned to face me, smiling sheepishly. "Sorry about that, Lauren," he said. "It *is* Lauren, right? You look just like your profile pic. I'd recognize that awesome hair of yours anywhere."

"Thanks." I reached up and touched my hair as if wondering if it was really still up there. "I mean, yeah, it's me. Um, hi?"

"I really appreciate you playing along. I was having trouble shaking those three without being an a-hole about it." He shot a look back at the club as if fearing those girls might come swooping out at any moment.

"Who, uh, who were they?"

He sighed, rubbing his face. "When I put that message up on Facebook, I never thought it would turn out like this," he said. "First I get tons of messages from random girls claiming to be the girl from the planetarium. And now some of them are actually showing up and, like, stalking me!"

"Um, yeah. That sucks," I said.

"Oh." He shot me a slightly confused look. "Right. I guess you responded, too, didn't you? But that's different." He waved a hand. "I mean, you just saw what I said about the Beast and figured you'd say hi, right? That's cool. Totally not the same thing, right?"

I blinked, taken by surprise. "Um . . ."

"Anyway, those girls obviously weren't the planetarium girl," he went on, too caught up in his own consternation to notice my confusion. "The dark-haired one actually tried to keep up the game, even after I told her she was way too tall to be the girl I was looking for. But the other two admitted pretty quickly that they just wanted to meet me." He shook his head. "I just don't get it."

Aw. I couldn't help finding it absolutely adorable that he was so flummoxed by all the female attention. Somehow, it made him even more attractive to know that he didn't even realize just how attractive he was.

"So they spotted you at the show and came over?" I asked, mostly to buy myself more time to figure out what to say.

"Actually, I posted something on Facebook earlier about coming to this show," he said. "I think they saw that and just showed up. Don't ask me how they got in—you and I were damn lucky to land tickets before it sold out."

Right. I smiled weakly, feeling like a big fat fraud.

His expression was rueful as he glanced down at me. "Pretty lame, right? I mean, it takes a special person to appreciate the Beast. And it was pretty obvious none of those girls had ever even heard of the band before tonight. Probably didn't even know where their name comes from."

"Quote from *Lord of the Flies*," I responded automatically.

He grinned. "My tenth-grade English teacher would be proud of you." Then his smile faded a little and he shook his head.

"Anyway, like I said, it was obvious that none of those girls were the one from the planetarium."

I nodded, knowing that Britt would want me to jump in and say something like, *Of course they're not that girl—I am! And I'll prove it!* and then grab him and kiss him like someone out of a movie . . .

I was so embarrassed just imagining myself doing anything like that that I almost missed what he said next. But when I realized he was staring at me expectantly, I blinked and dragged myself out of Embarrassing Fantasy Land.

"Um, what?" I blurted out.

"I said, how about some ice cream or something?" he said. "My treat. You know—to thank you for helping me escape just now. Plus, I'd love to chat about the show. None of my friends are fans, so it'd be nice to hang with someone who really appreciates the Beast like I do."

Some ice cream? His treat? A little neon sign went off in my brain, flashing OMG! OMG! OMG!

But I did my best to keep it casual as I responded. "Sure," I said. "Sounds like a plan."

"Cool. Come on, there's a good place just down the street. . . ."

The ice cream place he was talking about turned out to be less than two blocks away. On the short walk over we talked about our favorite MTIAB songs and the band's latest blog postings, and before I knew it we were walking into a cute little place called Chilly Milli's. I'd been there once or twice before; it had awesome homemade ice cream and was decorated with a bunch of pictures of penguins and icebergs and stuff. The place was pretty crowded even at that hour; there was a long line of people at the takeout counter, and several waitresses in sweet little sleeveless pink parkas were circulating among the dozen or so tables.

We found a free booth near the back. Once I was sitting there across from him, my brain suddenly went blank. He was staring up at the chalkboard listing the day's flavors, not saying anything.

"So," I blurted out, desperate to break the silence before it got awkward. "Um, weird how many girls responded to that post of yours, huh?"

Yeah, smooth, Lauren. Way to bring up the

one subject almost guaranteed to make things more *awkward.*

He glanced up at me, frowning a little. I could feel my cheeks going red.

"Pretty much, I guess." He didn't look totally comfortable himself all of a sudden. "I wrote that message sort of on impulse. See, right after I got home from that field trip, I was thinking about meeting that girl in the planetarium, and I ended up just sitting down and writing this awesome song called 'We Should Stop Meeting Like This,' and I was all psyched about it. So I was thinking about that girl, and wondering who she was and why she inspired me so much, and well . . ." He sighed. "The rest is history, I guess. I never did anything like that before, and I had no idea what would happen, you know? Guess I'm not sure how to handle it."

"That's cool," I said. "I mean, you know, not cool that they're stalking you or whatever. I mean, I understand. Not really; it's not like I've ever had guys show up wanting to meet me everywhere I went . . ." I trailed off, forcing a laugh and feeling like the world's biggest dork. "I just mean I hear you, I guess."

"Thanks. Anyway, enough about that;

I'd rather talk about the Beast," he said, obviously more than ready for the change of subject. And trust me, the feeling was mutual. "Did you see that crazy dude at the show?" he went on. "You know which one I mean."

"Uh, no." Great. Only like five minutes in, and I was already getting tangled in my own web of deceit. "Which crazy dude?"

"You know. Purple spandex? Crazy Mohawk?"

"I guess I didn't notice him." I was too distracted to come up with anything more creative. That was because a very interesting—and sort of scary—question had just popped into my head. Was this a *date*?

It was a totally foreign concept to me, at least firsthand. Oh, sure, Britt went on dates all the time, though she rarely called them that. She'd just say a guy had invited her to hang out, or that she was going to the movies with a dude she'd just met, or that she was going somewhere fun with a new hottie.

But I didn't really do anything like that. I'd never even been on a "first date" before—not really. Like I said, all two of my previous boyfriends had started out as friends. By the time we'd actually started going out together, things were pretty comfortable and casual between us, which made going out seem a lot less . . . well, datelike. The only other times I'd done anything at all like dating was stuff like school dances, which didn't really count and was usually more of a group thing anyway.

A first date. The whole idea seemed kind of weird and old-fashioned to me, like something out of a movie set in the 1950s or something. Or like my parents, who had a "date night" every weekend.

"Lauren?"

I realized I was drifting, not paying attention to what he was saying. "Oh!" I blurted out. "Um, sorry, I was just thinking about something. What did you say?"

He grinned. "It's okay. I'm always a little deaf myself after a Beast show. Think they're the loudest band in America, or what?"

"Probably." I couldn't help smiling back. "The first time I saw them live, I went home and started shouting at my parents because my ears were still ringing. They thought I was a total freak."

He laughed. "It's worth it, though, right?"

"Totally! I can't believe they're still only a local band. They're way better than most of the stuff on iTunes."

"Tell me about it. My little sister is always blasting this Top 40 garbage in her room." He made a gagging face. "And people say the Beast gives them a headache—that bubblegum crap is migraine city!"

After that, things got a lot better. Relaxed, even. A waitress showed up to take our order, and Riley started teasing me about ordering ginger ice cream. I didn't mind at all; I teased him right back about his choice to mix hazelnut gelato with mango sorbet.

Ice cream flavors aside, it turned out we had a lot in common. We spent the next half hour slurping up our sundaes and talking about everything and anything, from music to school to our families. I discovered that he was in a band called the Grovers with some other guys from his school, that he liked to go crabbing in the Chesapeake and mountain biking, and that he had a weakness for cheesy vampire movies; he coaxed me into admitting that I was afraid of the dark but loved snakes and other reptiles and had been begging my ophidiophobic dad to let me get a pet ball python for most of my life.

I even told him about my dreams to become a fashion designer. That was kind of a big deal, actually. I didn't talk to a whole lot of people about that, mostly because I was afraid they'd make fun of me. But Riley seemed perfectly willing to believe that I could do it.

I also learned that Riley had spent much of his childhood moving around the world with his parents, who both worked for the State Department. The family had lived in Germany, Brazil, Switzerland, and Lebanon before finally settling in the D.C. metro area when he was twelve.

"Luckily, I think this is it," he said. "The 'rents tell me we probably won't have to move again—their jobs now are both stateside."

I scraped a piece of crystallized ginger off the bottom of my bowl. "Wow, that's hard-core. I can't imagine moving around that much." I tried to picture what it would be like moving away from my hometown, my school, and the friends I'd had since kindergarten. "I've lived in the same place my entire life. Well, almost—we did move once, when I was seven, but only to a bigger house like three blocks away from the old one. It must be tough starting new schools all the time."

"Sort of." He shrugged. "But most of them were English-speaking schools for diplomats' kids and stuff, so we were all in the same boat. We pretty much knew how to get along with each other."

I gazed at him with new respect. "So did you have to learn all those different languages?"

"Technically, I probably didn't have to, since we usually lived in expat communities, and like I said, the schools were all in English. But I liked to at least give it a try." He chuckled. "It was a lot easier to pick things up when I was younger. So my Arabic still sucks, but my German and Portuguese are both pretty good."

"Really? Say something."

He grinned and let loose with a torrent of foreign words. It sounded totally cool and exotic.

"What's that mean?" I asked.

"It means I'm glad I ran into you tonight," he said, licking the last of his sorbet off his spoon. "This is fun. You're really easy to talk to."

"Thanks. So are you." I smiled at him,

feeling little pings of happiness going off in my brain. So was this what Britt felt every time she met a new guy? I kind of hoped not. Because this feeling was too special to waste on every other guy coming down the pike. I wanted her to find that one perfect guy . . . her own Riley.

Part of me couldn't believe I was falling so hard and fast for this guy. What had come over me? It was like I wasn't even the regular Lauren anymore, the cautious, reserved Lauren who preferred to test the waters, take it slow, get to know a guy as friends first. . . .

But the larger part of me was just glad I'd dredged up the guts to go over to Riley in the planetarium that day. Otherwise we might never have encountered each other, even though we only lived a few miles apart. And all of a sudden I couldn't stand the thought of never having met him.

Although I still hadn't come clean with him. Not really. I mean, sure, I'd told him I was Planetarium Girl in that first Facebook message. But ever since then I'd let him go on believing the conclusion he'd jumped to—that I'd just used that message as an excuse to contact him because of our shared interest in MTIAB.

And that didn't seem good enough. I wanted him to know that I really was The One.

Not that the truth was going to be easy. I'd seen how he reacted to the girls he thought were fakers. What if he thought I was one, too?

I'll be doing him a favor by telling him, I thought, trying to psych myself up. *If he knows he's found the real Planetarium Girl, it'll be way easier for him to blow off all the others, like the girls on Facebook and the ones at the club. . . .*

That finally convinced me. I had to do it. For Riley's sake. It was practically an act of charity.

"Listen," I said, setting down my spoon. "I want to tell you some—"

He wasn't paying attention. Suddenly he jumped to his feet, waving his own spoon over his head like a signal flag.

"Yo, Marcus!" he shouted. "Guys! Over here!"

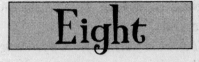

Eight

A bunch of people had just burst into the ice cream place and were waving and calling out greetings to Riley. At first they were milling around so much, shrugging off jackets and weaving their way between tables, that I couldn't tell how many of them there were. But eventually several crowded into the free seats in our booth, while the rest dragged over more chairs from nearby, and I could see that there were three girls and two guys.

"So how was the Maybe Who Gives a Crap show?" one of the guys demanded with a wide grin. He was a little shorter than Riley with sleek black hair, mischievous dark eyes, and a lean, tanned body that never seemed to stop moving. I also couldn't help noting with approval that he was wearing a superstylish Marc Jacobs printed shirt.

Riley laughed and rolled his eyes. "Remember how I was telling you my friends don't appreciate the Beast?" he told me. "Marcus here is the president of the anti-fan club."

"Hey, what can I say? They suck." The guy glanced at me, taking in my MTIAB T-shirt along with the rest of me. "Then again, if a hot girl like this actually tolerates them, I might have to rethink my opinion on that. Hello, beautiful. I'm Marcus." He stuck out his hand.

As I shook it, one of the girls let out a loud snort. "Don't fall for his Mr. Charming act," she advised me with a sly glance at Marcus. "He's a total hound."

"True," Riley said with a laugh. "Guys, this is Lauren. She's a fellow Beast fan I met on Facebook. We ran into each other at the show. Lauren, these are my friends—you already met Marcus, and that's Rachel." He gestured to the girl who'd spoken, a stylishly dressed redhead with a pointy chin and an intelligent face. "Over there is Jake, that's Haley, and, um . . ." He stopped as he glanced at the last of the girls, a petite blonde with her hair pulled back into a perky ponytail. She was wearing a pink spaghetti-strap tank that barely contained a truly impressive set of knockers.

"Nice to meet you, Lauren," Rachel said, while the others added hi's of their own.

All except for Marcus. He'd just jumped out of his chair and rushed over to the nameless blonde's chair, looking excited. "Dude," he said to Riley, reaching down and squeezing the girl's bare shoulders. "Surprise!"

"Uh, what?" Riley looked confused and a little wary.

Marcus laughed. "Don't look so suspicious, bro. It's good news. See, I finally tracked down the one and only Planetarium Girl for you! Voilà!" He stepped back with a sort of bow, gesturing dramatically to the girl in front of him.

She giggled. "Hi, Riley," she said with a cute little tilt of her head. "Nice to see you again. I didn't get a good look at you there in the planetarium, but I'm glad to see that you're just as cute as I thought."

Riley looked startled for a second, but he recovered quickly. "Oh, wow," he said. "Hi there. What's your name?"

"I'm Chelsea," the girl said. "But you

can call me Planetarium Girl if you want. Or you can call me The One. Just as long as you call me." She giggled again.

Geez. This girl had more lame pickup lines than Britt. I was guessing she got away with it because, like Britt, she was super hot. The rest of her body was just as amazing as her boobs, topped off by a pretty round-cheeked face with big blue eyes.

"Um, nice to meet you, Chelsea." Suddenly seeming to remember I was there, Riley shot me a look. "Guess I can finish the intros now. Chelsea, this is my new music buddy, Lauren."

"Hi," Chelsea said, though it was hard to tell if she was actually talking to me or not, since she never took her eyes off Riley.

I was glad that he was looking at her again now, since I suspected my own face might be giving away my reaction to the latest introduction. "My new music buddy," huh? Wow, romantic. Not.

"So am I the coolest or what?" Marcus demanded as he dropped back into his own seat. He grinned around the table, his gaze finally settling on me. "Not sure if you know about my man's recent heartbreak, Lauren. But see, he met this special girl on our last class trip and he's been desperately searching for her ever since."

"Yeah, so I heard." I was surprised at how normal my own words sounded. Did that mean I was getting more comfortable with my own lies? I wasn't sure I liked the thought of that.

"So Riley was so love-struck after meeting his mystery girl that he ran right home and wrote her a song—" Marcus cut himself off, spinning in his chair and leaning across the table to stare at Riley. "Hey, that reminds me. I told Chelsea here you were dying to sing that song for her. So how about it?"

"Not right now, bro." Riley smiled and shrugged as he glanced at Chelsea. "No offense. I just want to get to know you better before I get into that sort of thing. Hope you don't mind."

"Not at all." She reached up to adjust one of her straps, letting her hand linger near her cleavage. "I like a guy who wants to know a girl better before he gets into, you know, *that* sort of thing."

It was all I could do not to roll my eyes. No wonder he seemed willing to believe this imposter might be Planetarium Girl. She was full of clever lines like the one I'd somehow managed to spit out without thinking that day in the dark. Only, unlike me, she was actually capable of coming up with them in the light, too.

Meanwhile Marcus was shaking his head. "I told you," he said to Chelsea. "Dude's a hopeless romantic."

"I don't mind. When you find that one person you just can't stop thinking about, it's worth the wait." She reached over and touched Riley on the arm. He looked down at her hand, not seeming to mind seeing it there. Touching him.

I gritted my teeth. This "date"—or whatever it was—which had started out awkward and then turned awesome, had suddenly taken a steep downward dive into awfulness. For a second all I could think of was figuring out a way to extricate myself before I did something crazy, like jump up on the table and pound my chest like King Kong while shouting that *I* was the real Planetarium Girl. . . .

"So Lauren," redheaded Rachel said, turning to me as Chelsea continued to flirt shamelessly with Riley. "You're into music, huh? What else do you like besides Maybe There Is a Beast?"

I blinked at her. "Um . . . ," I began stupidly. Then my brain kicked back into gear. "I like all kinds of stuff. Rock, alternative, punk—the basics. Although my parents went through a major reggae phase a couple of years ago, and I actually still listen to Bob Marley sometimes."

"Really?" She laughed. "That's cool. I'm more into metal myself, but I like a lot of punk, too. . . ."

After that we kept on chatting, with the other girl, Haley, joining in once the topic turned to movies—apparently her favorite topic, since, as she informed me almost immediately, she wanted to be a filmmaker one day. Now and then Marcus and Jake jumped into our conversation as well, though they spent the rest of the time arguing with each other about sports.

But as cool and nice as they all seemed, I only managed to keep about half my attention on Riley's friends. The rest was focused on Chelsea, aka Ms. Fake 'n' Flirty, who was completely monopolizing Riley's attention. Every time I peeked over at them, she seemed to be touching him. Or smiling at him. Or leaning toward him so he could look down her shirt. Not that he actually did that. At least not while I was looking. But still . . .

Finally, after everyone had finished their ice cream, Marcus grabbed Haley's arm to check her watch. "Hey, there's a monster movie marathon on TV tonight starting at midnight. Who's up for watching at my house?"

"I'm there," Jake said. "But only if there's some of your mom's awesome butterscotch cookies."

Rachel laughed. "When have we ever gone to Marcus's and his mom *didn't* have those cookies waiting for us?" she said. "Anyway, I'm in too, but I can't stay too late. I have gymnastics in the morning."

"So it's a plan?" Marcus glanced around at the rest of us.

I seemed to be included in the invitation, but I hesitated before answering. It felt kind of weird to be heading off to hang at the house of someone I'd only met like an hour ago, even though Marcus and the rest of them all seemed totally normal and non-serial-killerish. Besides, I wanted to make sure Riley was going before I committed to anything.

Riley shrugged. "It's not a Beast concert,

but it beats homework," he joked. "I'm in."

"Me too!" Chelsea spoke up immediately. Then she giggled. "That is, if a non–Grove High person is allowed to come?"

"Any Planetarium Girl of Riley's is always welcome," Marcus replied with a grin. Then, seeming to remember I was there, too, he added, "Any music pals of Riley's too. You coming, Lauren?"

"Thanks, but I think I'd better pass." I stood up, visions of more annoying flirting dancing through my head. If Chelsea was already all over Riley in public, who knew how she'd be once they were tucked away in somebody's dark basement or wherever. I so didn't need to see that.

"Aw, you sure?" Rachel sounded genuinely disappointed. "You haven't lived till you've tried Marcus's mom's cookies."

Riley nodded. "She's like a baking genius. Come on, Lauren. It'll be fun."

I forced a smile. "Maybe next time."

They walked me back to my car over near the Cave Club. I had no idea where Britt had gone or how she and Todd had gotten home, but I wasn't too worried about it. Britt was nothing if not resourceful.

Riley hung back a little apart from the

others as I fished in my purse for my keys. "It was great getting to know you better," he told me quietly.

"Yeah, me too." I glanced up at him. He was looking back at me, his face sort of serious. For a second we just stayed there like that, looking at each other. Ping. Ping. P—

"Come on, Riley!" Chelsea raced over, ponytail and various other portions of her anatomy bouncing. "I can't wait to get to Marcus's house. I love monster movies—just promise you'll protect me if I get too scared!" Giggle, giggle, head tilt.

That was enough for me. Enough games, enough wondering what Riley was thinking about me, and *definitely* enough Fake Planetarium Girl.

"Night, everyone," I called out quickly. Then I jumped in my car, slammed the door shut, and gunned it out of the parking space without a backward glance.

Nine

Hi L!
Last night was fun, right? I'm still humming that "Crash" song the Beast debuted at the show. Btw, my friends all thought you were great. 2 bad you couldn't come to M's after ice cream. You fit right in like 1 of us. Glad we met up!
R.

I rested my chin on one hand, staring at the Facebook message from Riley. It was Saturday morning. I'd woken up from a dream about eating ice cream in Brazil and immediately started wondering how things had gone last night after I left. And the message left me wondering more than ever.

There was one way to find out what I wanted to know. I could answer the message and take it from there.

Hi Riley,

The Beast is always great. Meeting your friends was great, too. They're all really cool. Marcus kinda reminds me of my friend Britt — always trying 2 set peeps up w/each other, ha ha.

L.

There. I sat back from the keyboard. That should do it.

I only had to wait about thirty seconds before his answer came:

Marcus is a freak. He's always got something up his sleeve. That's what makes him so much fun, lol.

Hmm. He still wasn't mentioning Faker Girl. I skimmed the brief message again, trying to interpret what that meant. Was it a good sign? Or did it not mean anything at all?

Maybe it was time to stop with the games and just come out with it. I typed fast so I wouldn't chicken out.

So that Chelsea seemed nice. She really
seemed to like u a lot. Think she's really
P. Girl?

I hit send, then immediately regretted it. What was I doing? By asking that question I'd all but told him *I* wasn't Planetarium Girl. Which wasn't, you know, technically true or anything. So much for not playing games. . . .

Once again, he wrote back quickly.

Chelsea seems cool & all. But I'm not sure
she's really PG like she says. I remember PG
being taller, for 1 thing . . .

My fingers seemed to have a mind of their own. Before I knew it, I'd typed a quick response.

So what did u tell her?

This time the answer took a little longer to arrive.

I told her she was cool but I wasn't sure it was gonna work . . . I hate having 2 do stuff like that!!! Esp. b/c like you said, she seemed into me . . . Maybe I shouldn't be so quick 2 blow her off. But I really wanna give the whole PG thing a chance before I give up on it, u know? Not 2 sound corny or whatev, but it was like a special moment, and I don't want 2 just go out w/someone else and forget about it . . . Do I sound like a total dweeb???? haha, sorry 4 rambling on you . . .

I felt relief wash over me as I read what he'd written. So flirty floozy Chelsea was out of the picture already. Good.

Still, I couldn't help feeling kind of annoyed, too. If there really had been all those sparks between us that day at the planetarium, why couldn't Riley now see that *I* was the one he was searching for? I felt those same sparks every time I saw him. Why didn't he?

But I did my best to swallow back those feelings as I typed another response.

Ur not a dweeb. I think it's sweet. Why settle for less than what u want?

He wrote back again within seconds.

Thx, I needed 2 hear that. Marcus thinks I'm nutz to pass up a girl like that just b/c she's not "The 1," lol.

Yeah. I bet he did. Marcus seemed like the type not to miss any opportunity for a little romance . . . or whatever. I hadn't been kidding when I'd said he reminded me of Britt.

Just then the doorbell rang. Stepping over to glance out my window, I saw Britt on the front step. I paused on my way out of the room just long enough to send one last message:

Gtg, my bff is here. TTYL.

Then I ran downstairs to let Britt in. Meow Tse Tung was marching back and forth in front of the door, meowing insistently. Even though he lives the life of a pampered prince in our house, he's always up for adventure and is constantly doing his best to make a break for it. It's become pretty much automatic for all of us to grab him before we open the front door.

"Sorry, you're not going exploring today, Chairman," I said, scooping him up in one arm. Ignoring his yowls of protest, I swung open the door.

Britt knows all about Meow's fugitive tendencies too. She darted in and slammed the door behind her.

"Curses, your escape has been foiled again, little man," she said, tickling Meow under the chin.

He yowled once more, then started purring. I dumped him gently onto a chair. When I stood up, Britt was staring at me.

"So?" she demanded. "I'm dying of suspense here. All your text said was that you hung out with Riley for a while after I left. I want details, girl. Details!"

I sighed. "Oh, I have some details for you, all right."

She blinked, leaning closer to scrutinize my expression. "What's that face? That doesn't look like a happy blissed-out-in-love Lauren face. What happened? Did he turn out to have bad breath, stinky feet, an obsession with stamp collecting? What?"

She looked so frenetic that I couldn't help laughing a little. "Shut up already and I'll tell you. . . ."

On our way up to my room, I filled her in on everything, including the recent exchange of FB messages.

"So basically," I finished at last, "even though I had a great time with him last night—"

"At least before Boobsy McSlutterson showed up," Britt put in, nodding sympathetically from her position sprawled out on my bed.

"Yeah, that. Anyway, it's just totally frustrating. If he thought I was The One at the planetarium when I was tripping over my own feet and falling all over him in the dark, why can't he see it when I'm standing there in front of him? Especially since, like he pointed out himself, there aren't that many girls around who are so into the Beast. I mean, what the hell?"

"I don't know." Britt shrugged. "Guys are a mystery."

I raised an eyebrow. "Really? I thought you were the world's leading expert on the species."

"Oh, I totally am! But that doesn't mean I actually understand them. I just know how to make them behave." She grinned. "Sort of like a lion tamer or something." Then she went serious again. "The question is, babe, do *you* still feel those sparks? Because if you do, it's worth trying to whip that lion into shape."

I kicked back in my desk chair, staring at my laptop and feeling kind of moody. "Yeah. That's the crazy thing. After getting to know him better, I'm feeling more sparks than ever." I shrugged and glanced at her. "Which brings me back to my main question. Why doesn't he feel it too? Why can't he see that *I'm* the girl from the planetarium—or at least that I'm the one who's right for him?"

"It's not that simple," Britt said. "Guys are, like, total idiots about this kind of stuff. All you have to do is prove to him that you two are meant to be, and he'll come around. We just need a plan."

"A plan?" I echoed dubiously.

"Sure." Britt was lying on her stomach

with her feet sticking up behind her, and as her face went into thoughtful mode, her feet started waggling around—sort of like how Meow's tail twitches when he's pondering a pounce on my dad's toes.

I was thinking too. Mostly about how there had been enough game playing already between me and Riley.

"I don't know . . . ," I began.

"I've got it!" Britt sat bolt upright. "How about if I call and tell him you were in a terrible accident and you're in the hospital? That should shake him up and make him realize what you mean to him!"

"Ew, no!" I was horrified by the very thought. "What is this, my life or some cheesy soap opera? Besides, what happens if he does show up at the hospital and I'm not there?"

She shrugged, seemingly untroubled by my reaction. "Okay, then how about this?" she said. "We create a fake Facebook account and pretend to be one of the Planetarium Girl fakers. Then we arrange for our faker to meet him in some out of the way but totally romantic spot, like maybe the steps of the Lincoln Memorial or something. Then when she stands him up—of course, since she doesn't exist—and you happen to walk past at just the right time—"

"Are you kidding? This is me we're talking about here, not Drew Barrymore starring in some madcap, zany romantic comedy movie."

"So what? Maybe if you lived your life like a romantic comedy, you'd get more dates."

I rolled my eyes. "Look, the point is, I'm disappointed, but I'm not desperate. If Riley has decided for whatever reason that he doesn't want to be with me as more than a music buddy or whatever, I'll just have to deal." I sighed, my mind drifting to the way his arms had felt holding me in the planetarium, and then to our awesome conversation in the ice cream parlor. "It's just a shame this didn't work out. . . ."

Britt looked sort of annoyed. "So you're really just going to give up? Even after the sparks and everything?"

"I told you I didn't believe in love at first sight. Maybe this just proves I was right."

She glared at me for a second, looking sort of sullen. Then her expression cleared. "Okay, whatevs," she said with a wave of one hand. "If that's really the way you want to go, I'm with you. BFFs, right?"

"Right," I said, relieved for once that she had such a short attention span, especially when it came to guys.

"Then the next item on the agenda is cheering you up and helping you forget all about Mr. Planetarium What's-His-Name." She beamed at me. "And what better way to forget one guy than with another one? Better yet, a whole bunch of other ones?"

"What are you talking about?"

"Tonight's that party over in Silver Grove, remember? The one Tommo invited us to."

"Invited *you* to," I corrected. "I just happened to be sitting there."

She ignored that. "You saw for yourself that Tommo's superhot," she said. "I'm dying to get to know him a little better, see what he's all about. So how about it? Want to hit the Grove scene tonight and do some dancing?"

"Silver Grove?" I said. "That's where Riley lives. What if he's at the party? I don't want him to think I'm stalking him like one of those crazy posers from Facebook."

"Oh, right. I almost forgot Riley goes

to Grove too. Still, he and Tommo don't exactly seem like they'd hang with the same crowd."

Yeah. That was the understatement of the year.

"And anyway, if he does show, can't you just, like, avoid him or whatever?" Britt's voice took on a pleading tone. "See, Tommo's totally hot, but like you said yourself, he's maybe kind of nuts, too. If I'm going to this party, I'd rather have my wingwoman along just in case I need a handy excuse to cut out early, know what I mean?"

I hesitated, but only for a moment. This wasn't the first time Britt had asked me to play her sidekick at a party or other event. And normally I was happy to do it. That was what friends were for, right? So why should I let a guy—no matter how cute yet exasperating—come between BFFs?

"Okay," I said, trying not to let my reluctance show. "I guess I'm there."

Ten

I stared at myself in the full-length mirror on the back of my bedroom door. If I did say so myself, I was looking pretty great. My hair fell over my shoulders in glossy waves, my lips were sporting the latest hot shade of scarlet, and I'd put together a killer outfit: a sassy red-and-white print dress from my favorite vintage clothing shop on U Street, some cute ballet flats, and a few key pieces of funky jewelry.

As I surveyed my party-ready look, I did my best to quiet my nerves. Moving on was one thing. Was it a huge mistake to try to do it at a party in Riley's hometown? Different crowds or not, what if he *did* show up?

But I knew it was too late to back out

now. I couldn't leave Britt in the lurch, especially since I was more than a little dubious about Tommo's sanity myself.

"Plus, it would be a waste of an awesome look," I whispered to my reflection. I spun around to get all the angles, hoping to psych myself up. It worked—but only a little. Still, it was enough to get me moving out the door and down the stairs.

As I headed for the front door to watch for Britt, I saw my parents bustling around the kitchen, unpacking weird-looking ingredients from several shopping bags. They were laughing and chatting, and my mom was holding a glass of wine. Chairman Meow was weaving in and out between their legs, clearly hoping for a treat.

"Oh, right," I said. "It's date night."

My dad looked up from unpacking a bunch of bags of nuts and raisins and stuff. "That's right, Lauren," he said. "We're kicking off Moroccan week with some *ferakh maamer*. Want to join us?"

"Wouldn't that sort of defeat the purpose?" I leaned against the doorframe. "I mean, date night should be about romance." I shot a look at the raw chicken my mom had just taken out of its own bag. "Not that cooking up your own dinner and then hanging around the house seems all that super-romantic to me."

They both just chuckled and exchanged an amused look. Typical. What they called date night usually consisted of little more than staying home, cooking a meal of whatever exotic ethnic cuisine they'd chosen for the week, and then playing board games or looking through old photos or just hanging out and playing with Meow. Like I said, not exactly super-romantic in my book.

"You look nice tonight, honey," Mom said, taking in my outfit.

Dad nodded. "Looks like you're ready to go out dancing," he added.

"Thanks." I twirled to give them the full effect. "So why don't you two ever make date night a *real* date night? You know—get all dressed up in your best clothes, hit the town, go out dancing . . ."

Again they both chuckled. "Dancing? Us?" Mom said.

Dad did a funny little shuffle in his slippers. "Do any of the hot new dances call for two left feet?" he joked.

"I'm being serious," I said. "Why not give it a try?"

"We're just not 'going out' people, Lauren," my mother said with a smile, reaching over to give Dad's arm a fond squeeze. "Come to think of it, weren't you asking the other day how we got together? Because that's how."

"What do you mean?"

"She means that back in college, we were the two who always wanted to hang out at the dorm instead of hitting all the parties." Dad shrugged. "And even now, we still have the most fun just spending time together like this."

"Okay, if you say so . . . ," I said just as the doorbell rang. "That's Britt. See you later."

"Don't be too late," Mom called after me as I headed down the hall.

"And have fun!" Dad added. "Do some extra dancing for us!"

"Wow. When Tommo said half of metro DC would be here, guess he wasn't exaggerating," Britt said as she threw her car into park.

"At least not much," I agreed. We'd finally found a free space where Britt could wedge her car in between a Prius and a motorcycle. The rest of the leafy suburban block was completely packed with vehicles of all shapes and sizes. And it wasn't hard to tell where most of the drivers and passengers had gone. A stately Georgian-style house near the middle of the block was lit up like the Fourth of July, with loud music blaring out of every window. If the neighbors hadn't called the police already, I was sure it was only a matter of time.

Britt climbed out of the driver's seat, smoothing down her trendy cami top and sleek True Religions. She shot me a look across the top of the car as I got out too. "Ready to rumble?" she asked, looking eager and confident. As always.

"Sure, I guess." I was feeling anything but eager and confident myself. More like nauseated. My stomach had started doing flips as soon as we'd reached Silver Grove. I wasn't sure whether that was because I was afraid of running into Riley, or because I was hoping I *would* run into him. Frankly, the very possibility was giving me the major shivery chills.

When we reached the party house, the front door was standing wide open. Inside we could see throngs of teenagers mingling and having fun. Loud voices competed with the blaring music, and the air was rich with the scents of sweat, beer, and cologne.

Nobody paid much attention to us as we entered the foyer. Well, aside from the usual guys checking Britt out. She gets that everywhere she goes; I usually don't even notice it anymore. Although this time I couldn't help noticing that some of the guys were giving *me* the once-over, too. Yay for my awesome outfit!

"How are we ever going to find Tommo in this crowd?" I asked, speaking directly into Britt's ear so she could hear me over all the racket.

Britt shrugged. "He's not too hard to spot," she shouted back.

She had a point there. Tommo was the type of guy who'd be hard to miss even in the middle of a hurricane or something. We didn't see him in the formal living room off to the right, where a couple of hippie chicks were doing some sort of interpretive dance while a bearded guy with glasses played the ukulele. I wasn't sure how they heard him, since the hip-hop music from the next room was so loud it was making the whole house throb. But they seemed happy enough in their own little world. They didn't even seem to notice the couple making out on the sofa, or the kid drawing on his own arm with a marking pen, or the two teams of meatheads laughing uproariously as they winged Doritos at each other.

We pushed our way through all that to another room behind the first, where the music was even louder. That was because the house's expensive-looking stereo system was in there. It was hard to tell what the room's usual purpose was, since all the furniture had been shoved back against the walls to create a dance floor. At least two or three dozen people were currently bopping, grooving, grinding, and/or writhing to the beat while others were lined up around the edges to watch.

I took a look around, feeling sort of like some kind of explorer in a foreign land. It was weird to be at a party where I didn't recognize a soul. Or did I? I suddenly noticed a vaguely familiar blond head bouncing up and down at the far end of the room. I poked Britt on the shoulder.

"I think Tommo's over there," I shouted in her ear, hoping she could hear me over the wall of bass blasting out of the stereo.

Her eyes lit up as she looked where I was pointing. "Wish me luck!" she said.

At least that was my best guess at what she said, based on prior knowledge of her speech patterns and some rough amateur lip-reading. I smiled and nodded, patting the pocket in my skirt to indicate my cell phone, which was set on vibrate. We'd already agreed on a bunch of secret code words and stuff that she could use if she wanted me to come rescue her.

She pulled out a compact and quickly checked her face and hair, then hurried off. That left me alone in the sea of strangers. I glanced around, but there wasn't a familiar face in sight.

"Hey, sweetheart." A guy I'd never seen before paused to look me up and down as he passed. He seemed to like what he saw, since he added, "You look lonely. Want to make out?"

I rolled my eyes and shook my head. He shrugged and grinned, his body language saying, *Hey, it was worth a try.* Then he hurried off, shouting to some other guys who appeared to be playing basketball with a rolled-up sock and a large, fancy-looking Chinese vase.

Alone again among the many, I decided to try to find my way to the kitchen and help myself to a soda. It was already warm and stuffy in the house, and I had a feeling it could be a long night.

It wasn't easy crossing the dance floor, where a bunch of people were still dancing like spastic kangaroos. But then a different song came on, and I took advantage of the momentary confusion to dive across the middle of the room and through an arched doorway on the far end.

I found myself in what appeared to be the dining room. It was marginally less crowded in there; a few people were sitting at the mahogany table playing poker, while others were examining the books in a glass-fronted case on the far wall. Among the latter group I spotted a couple of familiar faces.

One was Rachel, Riley's cool female friend from last night. Another was Marcus.

I gulped. If they were here, that could only mean one thing. Riley had to be here too.

So now what?

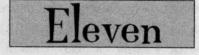

Eleven

As I was standing there frozen with indecisiveness, Rachel turned and spotted me. She looked surprised, then waved. Giving Marcus a smack on the arm to alert him, she made her way toward me around the table.

"Hey," I greeted the pair when they reached me.

"Hi, Lauren," Rachel said. "I didn't know you'd be here tonight."

I smiled ruefully. "I didn't either until my friend Britt talked me into coming." Hearing Britt's distinctive laugh during a brief break in the music, I glanced over my shoulder. I could see her through the archway. She was still back in the other room, tilting her head back to smile up at

Tommo. "There she is. Over there with the tall blond guy."

"You mean Tommo?" Marcus said. "How'd she get mixed up with that clown?"

"She met him on the field trip to the Smithsonian the other day."

"Oh, you mean you were on that trip too?" Rachel made a face. "Wasn't it a snooze?"

"Um, totally." I couldn't help being surprised for a moment. Didn't she already know I'd been on that field trip? After all, that was where Riley and I had met. . . .

But she wouldn't have any way of knowing that, I reminded myself. *Not unless they talked about me after I left last night, maybe. Because all he told his friends while I was there was that I was his new music buddy—he didn't say anything about me being Planetarium Girl. And as I've already figured out, he doesn't seem to want to believe that himself, so why* would *he mention it? His friends probably assumed we just met at the concert.*

"Have you seen Riley yet?" Rachel asked.

That yanked me immediately out of my own thoughts. "Um, no?" I said, my heart beating a little faster. "Is he here?"

"Marcus!" a girl shrieked, descending upon us like a banshee. She was grooving to the music, waving both arms over her head and shimmying her hips. "Come on, you gotta dance with me, baby!"

"How can I say no to a beautiful woman?" Marcus replied, immediately starting to wriggle his own hips as he allowed the girl to pull him off toward the other room.

As they disappeared into the mob on the dance floor, Rachel laughed and shook her head. "In case you haven't noticed, Marcus is the life of the party," she said.

"I noticed." I returned her smile, but I wasn't really thinking about Marcus. "Um, did you say Riley's here?"

"Yeah, somewhere." She cast a look around, then shrugged. "Haven't seen him in a while, actually. He's probably hiding out from the hordes of groupies that've been panting after him since he posted his little love quest on Facebook."

It only took one look at her wildly rolling eyes to guess what she thought of the fake Planetarium Girls. "That quest of his," I said hesitantly. "You know—for The One, or Planetarium Girl, or whatever . . ."

"'Whatever' being the operative word."

Her eyes were still rolling. "I can't believe he's serious about the whole thing. Especially after seeing some of the girls who've replied."

For a second I felt vaguely insulted. But I fought back the feeling. After all, she had no idea *I* was one of those girls. She was talking about the others: girls like the ones at the club, or like Chelsea. And thinking about that, I could see her point. Chelsea didn't exactly seem like Riley's type to me. At least I hoped she wasn't.

"So he's pretty serious about tracking down that girl, huh?" I did my best to keep my voice casual, light. Just party chit-chat. La di da.

Rachel leaned back against the dining table and sighed. "Unfortunately, it seems like it. Riley's pretty chill most of the time, but when he gets the idea in his head that he really wants to do something or whatever— look out. He won't let up until he gets what he wants, you know?"

"I guess this Planetarium Girl really made an impression on him?"

"I guess. Or it might just be that Riley's a hopeless romantic. And that he's refusing to accept that none of these so-called

Planetarium Girls are anywhere near good enough for him, at least in the not-so-humble opinions of me and all the rest of his friends." Rachel laughed. "Don't tell him I said that, though."

She was obviously kidding, but I crossed my heart anyway, once more reminding myself that she wasn't talking about me. Not really. "So you don't think he'll give up on Planetarium Girl anytime soon?" I asked.

"Doubtful. I totally heart the boy, but like I said, he can be way stubborn. Marcus and Haley said he hardly talked about anything else but that girl in study hall yesterday."

Just then someone called Rachel's name. I glanced over and saw a couple of people pushing their way toward us. She smiled and waved to them.

"I'll catch you later," I told her. "I'm going to get a drink."

"See you around," she replied, then hurried forward to meet her friends.

I slipped away into the kitchen. It was empty except for a couple of wildly giggling girls who appeared to be attempting to stuff a banana, some grapes, half a bottle of chocolate syrup, and who knew what else into the blender. Ignoring them, I rummaged around in the fridge until I found a Coke.

Then I wandered back out into the main room, my head spinning with the knowledge that Riley was somewhere at this party. What now? Should I look for him and say hi? Should I try to avoid him so he didn't think I was anything like those girls Rachel was talking about? Or should I maybe just leave and avoid the whole question?

I realized the last option wasn't really an option at all. For one thing I couldn't abandon Britt, especially since Riley's friends had all but confirmed that Tommo was a nut. Besides, I couldn't abandon her even if I'd wanted to. She was my ride. And at the moment she was nowhere in sight.

Somehow, though, I couldn't make myself feel disappointed. And if I was being honest, I knew why. Despite my resolution mere hours ago to give up on him, I wanted to see Riley again.

Maybe he's getting sick of all these shallow wannabes, I told myself as I wandered through one crowded room and then another. *Maybe tonight is when the magic finally happens again.*

When he realizes it's been me all along. . . .

I kept wandering. No sign of Riley. Or Britt. Or Rachel, Marcus, or anyone else I even vaguely recognized. I kept an *of course I'm having fun* smile pasted on my face even though I was starting to feel kind of stupid and uncertain again.

But by now I couldn't ignore the fact that I was dying to see Riley. And why not? He didn't seem to think I was a crazy stalker so far. Hadn't he messaged me on Facebook just that morning? That was a good sign, right?

I made my way through the room with the stereo and the dance floor, where I caught a glimpse of Riley's friend Jake slow-dancing with some girl. Britt and Tommo definitely weren't there anymore, and I couldn't see Marcus and his dancing friend, either.

Turning off to the side, I headed through a doorway and down a narrow hallway leading to more rooms at the back of the house. One of them was some sort of den-library combo, where a group of guys were watching a sports news show on a plasma TV. Another group of mostly guys was on the back screened porch. A few of them shot glances my way when I poked my head in there, and one beefy football type looked like he was thinking about coming over. I ducked back out and kept moving, not in the mood for flirting with random guys. Not that I was *ever* really in the mood for that. . . .

As I headed back down another hallway— the house was huge—I hit a staircase. There were voices coming from upstairs, but I kept moving past the stairs, not sure I wanted to go up there. Where the heck was Riley? I hadn't seen Rachel or Marcus in a while either. What if they'd all decided to leave?

"Hey, chica," a short, muscular guy said as I passed him just as he was coming out of a powder room. "What's your name?"

"Busy," I said, not stopping. Having so many guys checking me out or hitting on me did make me feel good about my outfit. Still, what was the point in looking good if the guy I really wanted to impress never even saw me?

As I rounded a corner I noticed a door standing slightly ajar. Glancing through it, I saw steps leading downward. The basement. Different music was drifting up from down there.

I took a step down and then hesitated,

hearing mostly female voices down there. Then a guy laughed. My heart jumped into my throat. I knew without a shadow of a doubt that it was Riley.

Taking a few deep breaths, I headed down the steps and found myself in a spacious basement rec room. It had a pool table, several huge leather sofas, a big-screen TV and PlayStation console, some ancient-looking Persian rugs covering the tile floor, and lots of framed advertising posters on the paneled walls. There was a gleaming mahogany bar along one wall, and next to that was an old-school jukebox.

There were probably fifteen people down there, but my eyes went immediately to one of them. Riley was standing beside the jukebox, leaning one elbow casually on its rounded top.

He didn't see me at first. For a moment all I could do was look at him as the usual feelings washed through me—soaring heart, pinging, and all.

Then the song that was playing ended. "Any requests?" Riley asked, leaning over the controls.

There was a chorus of giggles. "You pick, Riley!" a girl's voice exclaimed.

"Yeah," another girl said. "You have the best taste!"

"Is there any Maybe It's a Beast on there?" yet another piped in. "Because I love them even more than you do, Riley!"

I looked around. The pinging faded, and my heart sank. There were three guys playing pool over at the table, and another one rummaging around behind the bar. Aside from them—and Riley, of course—everyone else in the basement was female.

Two of the girls were busy playing Tomb Raider on the big screen, but the rest were buzzing around Riley like flies around a juicy piece of meat. Chelsea wasn't among them, though I did recognize one of the girls I'd seen at the club the night before. She looked sexy and ready for action in a skintight V-neck top and a microscopic miniskirt. Most of the others were similarly attired in their best skankwear.

I almost turned right around and left. How was I supposed to compete with all that? And more to the point, did I even *want* to? Rachel's words danced through my head: *He won't let up until he gets what he wants*. Did he really want one of these girls? Was he determined that one of them was his One True Love?

"Lauren! Hey, what's up?"

He had spotted me. I headed toward him, ignoring the stares of the other girls as they immediately zeroed in on me, clearly sizing me up.

"Hey," I greeted him, trying not to feel self-conscious.

"I didn't know you were going to be here." His smile made me forget everything else for a second. "What are you doing over here in Silver Grove again?"

"My friend Britt got invited to this party." I tried to sound casual and even a little bored. Okay, I hate playing games. But I hate seeming desperate even more.

"Cool." Riley waved a hand at the jukebox. "Any requests?"

I was becoming more and more aware of the stares—make that *glares*—from the other girls. "Um, I don't know. Let's see what we've got."

Turning my back on the glares, I leaned over the glass front of the jukebox. Riley leaned beside me.

"Let me guess. More Facebook friends?" I asked him quietly, tipping my head subtly back toward our observers.

His grimace showed clearly in the polished glass front of the jukebox. "Mostly," he whispered back. "The two over on the couch playing video games are friends of mine. They're sticking around to help rescue me in case I need to escape." He shot a quick look over his shoulder. "You know, Marcus would be in heaven with this many girls hanging around. But I have to admit it feels a little weird to me. I'm not exactly Mr. Casanova, you know?"

Again, adorable. Verging on adorkable. He just didn't know how amazing he was, did he? "Must be kind of awkward having them just show up everywhere you go," I said.

"Makes me want to stop updating Facebook about where I'm going," he agreed with a rueful chuckle. "Anyway, I'm glad you're here. Maybe you can help Jill and Casey keep me sane."

"Sure." I felt a rush of warmth, immediately followed by an unpleasant lurch in the pit of my stomach. On the one hand, it was cool that he already counted me in as one of his friends. But it only reinforced the fact that he clearly *didn't* see me as anything more. Let alone as The One.

I forgot about that as he put his hand on my arm. It was like a bolt of electricity shot through me at his touch, and for a second I sort of forgot to breathe.

He was pointing to one of the tunes in the jukebox. "How about that one?" he said. "Seems like your kind of vibe. Am I right?"

I did my best to focus on the words on the little card. The song he'd indicated was one of my favorites.

"You're so right," I told him, feeling a little breathless but doing my best to hide it. "You know me pretty well for someone who's only known me a week."

I'd meant it as a joke, one of those cute throwaway lines that Britt always produced so effortlessly. But maybe I didn't pull it off. In any case, he didn't crack a smile as he glanced over at me.

"Yeah," he said, his eyes thoughtful as they caught my own and held them. I stopped breathing again. "It's weird. I really do feel like the two of us are on the same—"

"Riley!" An impatient, giggling female voice interrupted, shattering the moment. "Hurry up and put on some music. You promised me a dance, remember?"

Twelve

I fell back a few steps, feeling as if I might hyperventilate. That moment between Riley and me had been brief but intense. What had the questioning look in his eyes meant?

I felt hopeful for a second. But only a second.

"Here, let's play this one!" The girl who had interrupted us, a toothy brunette with an obviously fake tan, punched a button on the jukebox. The strains of a treacly Top 40 ballad poured out of the speakers.

"Ugh," one of the girls on the couch said, looking up from her PlayStation controller. "Did you pick this piece of crap, Riley? Lame."

Riley shot her a sheepish smile and shrug, but Tanny McTannerson ignored the comment. "Come on," she ordered, grabbing him by the arm. "Let's dance."

Apparently, to her, "dance" was pretty much synonymous with "grind." She pushed herself up against Riley until you couldn't have fit a sheet of tissue paper between them. He looked a little uncomfortable but made no move to push her away.

I didn't want to watch but was too horrified to turn away. It was like a train wreck—a terrible, bloody train wreck with lots of casualties. As I stood there frozen in place, another girl came over to stand beside me. This one was a cute redhead in a form-fitting halter dress.

"I can't believe how pushy she is," the redhead commented, staring at Riley and the brunette.

"Yeah, me either," I said numbly.

The other girl looked me over. "My name's Kelsey," she said. "Who are you? One of Riley's friends from Grove?"

What was the point in lying? All of a sudden I was feeling pretty tired of pretending to be someone I wasn't. Or maybe that should be pretending *not* to be someone I *was*.

"No," I told the other girl wryly. "I'm the girl from the planetarium."

Kelsey rolled her eyes. "Aren't we all, sweetie."

Another girl had just wandered close enough to overhear us. She let out a sniff, looking me up and down.

"*You're* trying to pass yourself off as Planetarium Girl?" she said. "Get real. If you're going to be serious about this, at least you could cut your hair or pull it back or something."

"Good point," Kelsey agreed with a nod. "Everyone knows that Planetarium Girl didn't have all that crazy long hair."

"They do?" I said, perplexed.

The second girl stared at me as if she'd just realized she was talking to a complete moron. "Riley posted an update about that this morning. Didn't you see it? I guess he's trying to weed out the fakers. . . ." She paused to glare around at all the other girls in the room. "So he put down everything he remembered about her. Like how tall she was—about five foot six or so . . ."

Kelsey narrowed her eyes, looking the other girl up and down. "Yeah. Come to think of it, you look a little short to be Planetarium Girl yourself. Sure there's not something you want to confess?"

The other girl ignored her. "And that her hair seemed kind of short and sleek from what he could tell in the dark and all." She patted her own dark brown pixie cut.

My hand wandered up to my own long, wavy locks. For one crazy, confused second I wondered if this was all a big misunderstanding—if Riley had met some other, short-haired Planetarium Girl that day at the museum. . . . It would certainly explain why he was so certain I wasn't her. . . .

Then I remembered. I'd had my hair pulled back into a bun because of that stupid cockpit experience. Duh. It hadn't seemed like a particularly important detail at the time. But now I wondered if my long, wavy hair was what was holding him back from seeing that I was the real Planetarium Girl.

I've got to go tell him! I thought frantically, my gaze shooting back to Riley.

He was still dancing with Ms. Fake Tan. I couldn't see his face, only hers. Her eyes were closed, and her orange-tinted face wore a blissful expression. She still had her body pressed up against him and was now running the tips of her fingers up and down his spine in time to the slow beat of the song.

What was I doing? Suddenly I felt like the world's biggest loser. Here I was, all dressed up and looking my best, mooning over a guy who clearly didn't see me *that* way at all. Talk about pathetic. . . .

"Excuse me," I said to the other two girls, who had just started arguing with each other about how tall they were. "I've got to go."

I turned to make my way toward the stairs, wanting nothing more than to find Britt and escape before I turned into an entirely different person. A desperate, needy person who was throwing herself at a guy because of a few pings and a BFF with romantic delusions.

When I was halfway to the stairs, the song ended. Riley pulled away from Orange Glo Girl and looked around, spotting me right away.

"Yo, Lauren," he called, hurrying over.

What could I do? I didn't want to be rude or anything. So I stopped, turning to face him with a forced smile.

"Hey," he said, skidding to a stop in front of me. "Um, are you having fun?"

"This is quite a party," I hedged.

He laughed. "Yeah. Mikey's parents go out of town a lot, and he never fails to throw a kick-ass bash." Running one hand through his dark hair, he glanced around the rec room, an uneasy expression wandering briefly across his face. "This one's maybe a little weirder than most, though."

I wasn't sure what to say to that. For one crazy second I was tempted to channel Britt and just blurt out something blunt, maybe along the lines of *Hey, doofus, it would be a lot less weird if you'd get your head out of your butt long enough to see that I'm the girl you're looking for. . . .*

Before I could decide whether I had the guts to actually say something like that, I heard a chorus of giggles from over by the jukebox. A moment later another song started; it was another slow jam. At least this one didn't suck as hard as the previous song. In fact, I kind of liked it.

"My turn!" Kelsey sang out, hurrying over. Completely ignoring me, she started pawing at Riley. "Come on, sexy. Let's dance."

Riley smiled, looking uncomfortable. "Uh . . ." He shot a look at his two female friends, but they were bent over their controllers and completely caught up in their game.

"What are we waiting for?" Kelsey

stretched up, draping her arms over Riley's shoulders. "The song's half over!"

Riley did a quick little sidestep, neatly escaping from her embrace. "Maybe later, okay?" he told her with a winning smile. "Sorry. But I already promised Lauren she could have this dance."

Kelsey looked just as surprised as I felt. Before I knew what was happening, Riley had taken me by the hand and pulled me gently after him to an open spot in front of the jukebox.

"Sorry about that," he whispered as we started to dance. "I just couldn't deal with another one of them right now."

"N-no problem," I stammered, too busy focusing on the way his arms were wrapping around me to spit out anything more coherent than that. It was making me flash back to that moment in the planetarium when I'd crashed into him and felt those same arms hold me. Did he feel it too?

Apparently not. He was peeking over my shoulder at the other girls. I could only imagine the looks they were giving us, especially Kelsey. . . .

"Guess I owe you double for saving me," he said quietly. "You're a sport, Lauren."

That brought me down to earth with a thud. A sport. Yeah. Just what I wanted to hear from him.

"At least this time those girls picked a better song," I commented, determined to hang onto my dignity if at all possible. And the best way to do that was to survive this dance and then leave before I had some kind of pathetic emotional meltdown in front of him.

He nodded. "I like this one too." He started humming along with the music.

That distracted me from my angst. "Wow, you have a good voice," I said.

"Thanks." He smiled down at me, then switched from humming to actual singing, crooning the words into my ear. I felt a shiver start somewhere around my ear canal and travel through my entire body.

This time he seemed to feel something, too. Still singing softly, he tightened his hold around my waist, pulling me closer. Then he went back to humming again, swaying more and more slowly.

I could feel his heart beating against my body. His hands started moving, tentatively exploring my back. Was something happening here?

When I tilted my head back to look at him, I found him already staring down at me. Our eyes met, and once again I saw a question in his. I just held his gaze, not really caring much about the whole Planetarium Girl thing right then.

He wet his lips, and his eyes fell shut for a second. Then he opened them and started moving his face closer to mine. My lips parted of their own accord, already tingling in anticipation of the kiss. . . .

"Hey, everybody!" A sudden commotion over by the stairs drowned out the music.

Riley jumped back. He didn't quite let go of me, but the spell was definitely broken. I was left with dry lips, a pounding heart, and a racing mind. When I looked over at the stairs, I saw Marcus bounding toward us.

"Dude," he exclaimed, pounding Riley on the back. "Is this a party, or what?"

Riley gulped, then barked out a quick laugh. "You run out of girls upstairs, or what?" he asked Marcus. "I don't want you to, like, go into withdrawal or anything. Why don't you cut in, bro? Lauren's a good dancer."

He stepped back. Marcus moved forward

to take his place, holding out his hands to me with a smile. He said something—probably something witty and charming. But I had no idea what it was.

That was because I was too busy watching as Kelsey swooped in and grabbed Riley. He turned away to dance with her, not quite meeting my eye.

It seemed that the Moment—if that was what that had been—was over.

Thirteen

The next few minutes passed in a haze. Before I knew it, I'd danced with Marcus for several songs. After the first one they were all fast songs. Riley had somehow extricated himself from Kelsey and was once again controlling the jukebox.

I kept sneaking looks at him over there, but he wasn't looking my way. In fact, he wasn't really looking at anyone. He was keeping his head down, poring over the jukebox's song list as if it held the meaning of life.

What was he thinking? Had he felt what I'd felt while we were dancing? I was pretty sure that he had. In fact, I was 99.9 percent confident that he'd been on the verge of kissing me when Marcus had interrupted. So why was Riley acting like this now? Why had he made a break for it as soon as he got the chance?

At first such questions were wistful. But the more I turned them over in my head, the more annoyed I got. Riley wasn't stupid. So why couldn't he just get over himself and admit that I was the real Planetarium Girl? Surely he was smart enough to figure out the hair thing on his own. . . .

Luckily, Marcus didn't seem to notice how preoccupied I was, or at least if he did notice he didn't care. He was a good dancer and seemed to be enjoying himself. He grabbed my hand and spun me, then dropped me again and did a little spin of his own.

"Nice moves," I said, finally focusing on him.

"Thanks. You're not so bad yourself." He twirled me around one more time. "By the way," he added in a too-casual voice, "I've been meaning to ask you. What's the deal with your cute friend?"

For a second I thought he was talking about Riley. I almost blurted out something stupid to that effect.

But I caught myself just in time. "Wait," I said. "What cute friend? You mean Britt?"

He nodded. "The girl you came with. You pointed her out earlier, remember?"

Now that he mentioned it, I had. Britt's name had come up while I was talking to him and Rachel in the dining room.

"I know you said she came here to meet Tommo," Marcus went on. "Do you know if she's, like, serious about him?"

I was surprised. Only not. Guys always went for Britt. Why should this one be any different?

"Um, no," I told him. "She's definitely not that serious. They only met like a week ago."

"Oh! Cool. So do you know what her type is?"

The song ended and I stepped back. "She doesn't exactly have a type," I told him. "Go talk to her. I'm sure she'd love to meet you. You can tell her I sent you if you want."

I couldn't help smiling as Marcus thanked me and took off. It figured. Hadn't I thought all along that he reminded me of Britt? I couldn't imagine what Britt was going to do with the male version of herself, but I was looking forward to hearing all about it later. If only I had something equally fun and juicy to tell her about my own evening. . . .

I glanced around for Riley. When I found him, I caught him staring back at me. My heart gave a little jump when I saw the serious look on his face.

Enough is enough, I told myself firmly. We need to just deal with this already. I've got to stop playing games and lay it on the line, tell him—again—that I'm The One he's looking for. And not stop telling him until he believes it.

Summoning up all the courage I could find, I headed toward him. He was still watching me, not moving.

"Where is he?" a female voice cried out from the stairs. "Where's my sweet baby Riley? Because his Planetarium Girl is here at last!"

All eyes turned toward the newcomer, including mine. A girl was hurrying down the stairs. She had wide, teddy-bear-brown eyes, a big, round booty encased in a tight skirt, and a freakishly high-pitched voice. Her shoulder-length platinum hair was pinned back from her face with sparkly clips, and the heels of her wedge slides added about four inches to her petite height. Think a blond Betty Boop on steroids. Another girl, taller and a little less flashy in general, was right behind her.

The first girl spotted Riley just as she reached the bottom of the steps. She stopped short and clutched at her own heart.

"Oh my God," she exclaimed, her voice approaching a pitch that only dogs could hear. "It's you. It's really you! After our wonderful, romantic, inspiring meeting in the planetarium, I was afraid I'd never find you again!"

"Get in line, sister," one of the other fakers called out. "You're not the real Planetarium Girl. I am!"

The newcomer ignored her. She raced over and flung both arms around a surprised-looking Riley. "It's so awesome to see you again, Riley. I'm so glad you posted that thingy looking for me on MySpace."

"It was on Facebook," one of the video-game-playing girls called out, already sounding kind of bored. "Riley doesn't do MySpace."

"Whatever." The spawn of Betty Boop didn't seem too concerned. She never took her eyes off Riley as she went on. "Anyway,

I'm glad I can finally tell you that my name is Tiffie. And since you said you wrote me a song, I decided to write you one, too! Can I sing it for you, baby?"

"Um, sure, I guess." Riley seemed nonplussed.

Tiffie took a deep breath, then burst into song. It was a fairly tuneless, rambling thing with goofy lyrics about kindred souls and planetary alignment. I had to give her an A for creativity, though her singing voice rated about a D-minus. I guess everyone was too surprised to do anything but listen to the entire song—all three verses. Even Riley's friends put down their PlayStation controllers and turned to watch.

By the end almost everyone was laughing, including Riley. Tiffie didn't seem to mind. She beamed at him.

"See?" she said. "We inspired each other."

"That's cool." Riley seemed amused. "I, um, appreciate you laying it on the line like that, Tiffie."

The rest of the faker gang seemed pretty skeptical of the whole thing. "You can't be Planetarium Girl," one of them told Tiffie. "You're way too short."

"Oh, but she totally is!" I'd almost forgotten about the second girl, the one who'd been behind Tiffie on the steps. But now she hurried forward. "See, I was there, too, and I saw the whole thing."

"You couldn't have," Kelsey said bluntly. "It was dark, remember?"

"Of course she doesn't remember that, because she wasn't there," one of the others called out. "But I was. Because *I'm* Planetarium Girl."

Tiffie's friend clasped her hands in front of her. "It was super-romantic," she said. "See, we'd noticed Riley before the lights went out. It was totally love at first sight for Tiffie, you know? She was just going over to say hi when everything went dark. And, well, the rest is history."

It was so close to what had actually happened that I was taken aback. I glanced at Riley, who was slowly edging away from both of them.

Meanwhile the other fakers seemed unwilling to let Tiffie's story stand unchallenged. A skinny blonde jumped forward.

"That's not how it happened at all!" she cried. "See, I'd been checking out Riley all day. So I was right behind him in the planetarium, and I waited until it was dark so I could talk to him without any teachers interrupting us."

"Get real." My good pal Kelsey was the next to speak up. "You guys all sound like stalkers. No, the way Riley and I really met in the planetarium was just fate. I didn't even know what he looked like when I bumped into him in the dark; I just knew we were destined to be together."

"Oh yeah? Then how'd you know to ask him about that band on his shirt?" another girl challenged.

Kelsey's face went as red as her hair. "Oh," she said. "Um. I, well, uh . . ."

I was still hanging back behind the rest of the crowd watching the whole crazy scene. When I glanced Riley's way again, I was startled to find him sidling in my direction. He stopped right next to me.

"Can you believe this?" His voice was quiet and he sounded kind of weary. "When I started this, I was just looking for the girl who inspired me to write that song."

"Well, you're looking at her right here," I blurted out before I could stop myself. When I saw him blink in surprise, I gulped. But what the heck. It was too late to take it back now. "Like I tried to tell you from

the start, *I'm* the girl from the planetarium."
I kept my voice low so the others wouldn't
overhear. Not that there was much chance
of that at the moment. The competing fake
backstories were reaching a fever pitch. "I'm
the one you met that day, even if you don't
realize it."

His mouth twitched into an uncertain
smile. "Come on," he said, his voice crack-
ing a little. "I know you said something like
that in your first message, but I didn't think
you were really one of *them*."

"I'm not," I said. "I don't want to play
games; I was just telling the truth. Why do
you think I friended you in the first place?"

He shrugged. "I figured you saw that I
liked the Beast and were just joking around
about the other stuff as an excuse to get
in touch." Shooting a look at the arguing
fakers, he added, "I didn't think you were
like the rest of them."

I wasn't sure what else to say. Before I
could figure it out, shouts and the sounds of
running feet came from upstairs. The faint
cries of "Fight! Fight!" got everyone's attention.

The video game girls jumped up. "Uh-oh,
wonder what's up?" one of them exclaimed.

"Come on, let's go see!" Was it my imagination, or did Riley seem kind of relieved to have an excuse to rush away?

I frowned, but there wasn't much else I could do about it. Everyone was already racing for the stairs.

Following more slowly, I emerged upstairs just in time to hear the crash of breaking glass. "Take that!" a voice yelled.

A familiar sounding voice. Uh-oh . . .

I pushed my way forward through the chanting crowd. In the middle of the circle Tommo and Marcus were facing off against each other. Tommo's hair was soaked, and there was a rose petal stuck to his cheek. The rest of the bouquet was lying in a puddle on the rug, along with the remains of what had probably been a pretty nice vase.

"Stay away from her, buddy boy," Tommo snarled. "She's here with me."

Marcus danced away, easily dodging the punch as the taller guy took a swing at him. "Oh yeah?" he taunted. "Funny, she didn't say anything about that while we were making out just now."

Tommo let out a howl of rage and dove at him. Once again Marcus jumped out of the way, grinning from ear to ear as if he was having a blast.

Britt was there too, of course. She was wringing her hands and calling out for both of them to stop. But I knew her well enough to be able to tell that she was secretly thrilled to have two guys fighting over her.

I rolled my eyes and sighed. Typical. Then I shoved my way forward until I reached her. "Hey," I said. "What's new?"

"Not much." She smirked at me. "Some party, huh?"

"Yeah. But I think it might be time for us to make an exit." I tossed a glance at the guys, who were circling each other like a couple of prizefighters. Skinny, well-dressed prizefighters. "Always leave 'em wanting more, right?"

Britt looked amused. "See? You do listen to my words of wisdom! And you're right— let's get out of here."

"Right behind you." I searched the crowd for Riley as we pushed our way toward the door. But he was nowhere in sight.

Fourteen

"Up for some shopping, Lauren?" My dad poked his head into the den. "Mom and I are heading into the city to check out a new Asian market we heard about. We could stop somewhere for ice cream or sushi or something if you want to tag along."

I glanced up from my Spanish textbook. "No thanks. I'm not in the mood."

"But you're in the mood for *estudio del español*? On a beautiful Sunday morning?" Dad chuckled, gesturing to my book.

"Not really." I smiled weakly. "But I've got a test on Thursday, and I haven't even started learning the vocab yet."

"Okay. Far be it from me to discourage you from getting a jump start on your homework. If I did that, they'd take away my teacher's license." He winked at me. "We'll be home in time for dinner."

I kicked back on the love seat and stared at my textbook as I listened to him and Mom get ready to go. They called out one more good-bye, I heard a yowl as one of them chased Meow away from the door, and then the house went quiet.

Maybe I should have gone with them after all, I thought listlessly. It might have shaken me out of my funk. I'd been in a bad mood all morning. I wasn't usually the moping type, but I definitely was today.

Leaning over my textbook again, I did my best to focus. But the English translations looked just as incomprehensible as the Spanish words. With a sigh I tossed aside the book. What I'd told my dad was true, but I just couldn't concentrate on Spanish vocabulary right then.

Instead I grabbed my laptop, which I'd left on the coffee table, and checked my e-mail. Nothing interesting. I thought about going to Facebook but decided to pass. I definitely wasn't in the mood for a bunch of chatty, bubbly posts about everyone's fabulous Saturday nights.

I stood up and turned on the stereo. My iPod was in the speaker dock, so I scrolled through until I found one of my favorite new songs. Then I grabbed my sketch pad off the coffee table. I'd been working on some designs for prom dresses that *didn't* look as if they'd been designed by a mentally challenged chimpanzee raised in a Victoria's Secret store. But after the third time I had to erase the same neckline, I realized I wasn't going to be able to focus on that today either. Muttering a curse under my breath, I tossed the pad aside, feeling annoyed with myself. Why couldn't I shake off what had happened last night?

"Come here, boy," I called as Meow Tse Tung wandered into the room, tail at the alert.

I spent the next few minutes lounging on the couch, wriggling a piece of string for the cat to chase. Meow batted at it a few times, then yawned widely and stretched. Jumping up onto the coffee table, he started licking his paw.

I dropped the string and watched him, trying not to think about anything else. After the past few days of craziness, my brain was tired. And where had it gotten me? Exactly nowhere. Whatever Britt might think, it so wasn't worth it.

My laptop let out a beep. With a groan, I hoisted myself to my feet and went over to check it. It was an e-mail from Facebook. A new message from Riley.

> Hey Lauren! Just checking to make sure
> we're cool. Things got a little weird before u
> left last night, & I rly hope ur not mad??

I frowned. He rly hoped I wasn't mad? Was that all he had to say after basically calling me a liar? Suddenly I wasn't in the mood for *him*, either. My fingers flew over the keys.

> Weird? Is that what you call it? B/c I call it
> being totally blind 2 the truth. I told u I'm
> the real PG, & if u don't want 2 believe it
> that's ur problem. But don't tell me not 2 b
> mad about it!!!

I paused, letting the cursor hover over the send button. Maybe the response was a little harsh. Was it fair to take my bad mood out on him? Even if it *was* pretty much his fault. . . .

Highlight. Click. Delete. But I had to say something, right? I started typing again.

Don't worry. Not mad. All is cool. Rly.

"There," I told Meow as I sent the new and improved message. "Much more tactful, right?"

The cat stopped washing his paw long enough to stare at me, his long tail twitching. Then, with the equivalent of a kitty shrug, he returned his attention to his bath.

"Typical," I said, smiling despite my foul mood. "You're just another guy too wrapped up in your own thing to pay attention, huh?"

The laptop beeped again. Riley had written back.

Are u sure? I rly want 2 stay friends w/u no matter what.

I rolled my eyes, suddenly over all this back and forth. What was the point? He'd made it pretty clear last night that he didn't believe I was Planetarium Girl. Or maybe that he didn't *want* me to be Planetarium Girl. Maybe what he really wanted was someone breathless and giggly, like Tiffie or Chelsea or any of the other assorted fakers. At this point it was hard to come to any other conclusion.

The phone rang. For a second my heart jumped, and I was sure that it was Riley calling to tell me I was wrong about that, that he'd finally come to his senses and realized I really was The One. But when I checked caller ID, I saw that it was only Britt.

"Hey," I said dully as I picked up the phone.

"What's wrong?" she asked. "You sound weird."

I sighed into the phone. "I'm just in a cranky mood. You know—last night."

Britt clucked sympathetically. During our drive home I'd told her all about everything that had happened between me and Riley at the party. For once she hadn't had much advice for me, though she'd promised to help me figure out what to do.

The problem was, I was starting to wonder if I really wanted to *do* anything. Maybe it was better to pull back a little, let this ridiculous situation die a natural death.

"I always told you there was no such thing as love at first sight," I told Britt now. "Guess this proves it, huh?"

She didn't exactly answer that. "Want me to come over?" she asked instead. "You know I'm always happy to help you wallow. Or try to cheer you up, if you'd rather."

"Thanks." I felt marginally better just knowing she was there for me. No matter what. "I'm okay. I think I just want to hang out by myself for a while."

At that moment Meow stood up, stretched, and let out a sudden howl. I smiled.

"Well, not exactly *alone*," I said.

Britt laughed. "Okay. But call if you change your mind, okay? I can be there in five minutes."

We hung up, and I sat there staring at the phone for a second. As tempting as it was to let Britt come over and jolly me out of my mood, I really did want to be alone to try to figure out why I was letting this guy get to me so much. It wasn't as if he was my boyfriend or some longtime crush or anything. When you got right down to it, I barely knew him. I'd first laid eyes on him less than a week ago, and I hadn't really stopped obsessing over him since. If I didn't know better, I'd almost think I really was starting to fall for all that love-at-first-sight garbage.

I was still pondering that a few minutes later. Meow had moved from the coffee table to the couch beside me and was splayed out on his back so I could rub his belly. Suddenly the doorbell buzzed. The cat leaped straight up into the air, letting out a wild shriek and then dashing under my dad's favorite chair.

"Chill, dude," I told Meow with a laugh. "It's probably just Britt."

It would be just like her to come over anyway. I headed for the door, not totally disappointed. Maybe she could help me figure things out. I certainly wasn't getting anywhere on my own.

Hurrying into the front hall, I grabbed the door and swung it open. "Hey," I began with mock anger. "Didn't you hear what I—oh."

It wasn't Britt.

"Hey," Riley said with a sheepish smile, shuffling his weight from one foot to the other. "Hope you don't mind me stopping by like this. I was over this direction anyway, and your address was in Google, and, well, I just thought maybe we should talk or something."

I just stood there in the doorway, totally agog and not quite believing he was really here. What was he doing here? My mind reeled with the possibilities.

"Mroh-wohwww!"

The yowl yanked me out of my stupor. I let out a gasp, glancing down just in time to see a furry gray-and-cream form streak past my feet and straight out the door.

Fifteen

"Meow! Come back!" I cried, forgetting all about Riley in my panic.

How could I have been so careless? I knew better than to stand there like a dork with the door wide open. If anything happened to that crazy cat, it would be all my fault.

"Was that a cat?" Riley asked.

"Yeah." I hurried forward to the edge of the front steps and desperately scanned the shrubbery out front. But Meow had already disappeared. "His name's Meow, and he's a total spaz. He's not supposed to go outside."

"Gotcha." Riley was instantly all business. "Come on, let's find him—he can't have gone far yet."

Just then I spotted a flash of gray beneath an azalea. "There he is!" I said, pointing. Then I rushed forward and flung myself to my hands and knees, ignoring the way the moistness of the mulch seeped instantly into my favorite capris. "Here, kitty kitty!" I called softly, trying to keep the panic out of my voice. "Come on, baby. Here, Meow!"

"I think I see him," Riley called softly from somewhere behind me.

Glancing back, I saw him staring toward a clump of evergreen bushes along the property line. I winced as a car drove by out front, moving way too fast for the residential street.

"Meow!" I called, hurrying toward the bushes. "Are you in there, boy?"

By the time I reached him, Riley was already crouched down in front of the evergreens. "There," he said quietly, pointing. "He went that way."

"At least he's heading for the backyard instead of the street," I commented, grateful for small favors.

"How about if you go that way," Riley said, gesturing in the direction Meow had gone, "and I'll circle around the other side, try to head him off. Is he friendly?"

"Oh, yeah," I said with a small smile twisted with worry. "He's practically a Labrador retriever."

Riley nodded, pausing just long enough to reach out and give my arm a gentle squeeze. "Don't worry, we'll get him," he said. Then he turned and hurried off toward the far side of the house.

I stayed low to the ground as I moved along my side, keeping a lookout under the bushes. "Meow?" I called out as I turned the corner into the backyard. "Come back inside and I'll give you some nice, smelly tuna!"

I thought that might attract his attention. Dad always swears that Meow has a bigger vocabulary than most of his middle school students. I don't know about that, but Meow definitely does recognize at least a few words, "tuna" being first on the list.

There was a flash of movement across the yard. But when I spun to look that way, I realized it was only Riley. He saw me looking and gave a little wave, then crouched down again, creeping along and peering under every bush.

I went back to doing the same. The backyard was pretty small, consisting mostly of a vaguely Japanese-style rock garden that Dad had installed himself. Between the bushy mini maples, the hand-stacked rock formations and store-bought sculptures, and the holly bush badly in need of pruning, there were still plenty of places for a runaway feline to hide.

Then I spotted Meow. He wasn't exactly behaving like a fugitive. In fact, he was strolling across the little stone bridge spanning a rock "stream" as if he didn't have a care in the world.

I lunged toward him. "Meow!" I cried. "Hold still . . ."

"Ra-wohwww!" Meow saw me coming and jumped off the side of the bridge. He trotted along just fast enough to keep out of reach, zigzagging around a Buddha statue and a small stand of bamboo. Based on the soft yowls he was emitting, I had no choice but to think he was laughing at me, cat-style.

"Stop, damn it!" I called, fear and frustration making me feel like crying. "Meow, just come on already!"

He turned sharply to the left, making a beeline for the hedge separating our yard from the neighbors'. I gulped, suddenly remembering that they had a bad-tempered little terrier who was always chasing the neighborhood strays. Meow was so ridiculously friendly; what if he decided to make friends with the little beast and got chomped?

I stumbled over a stone, almost wiping out. As it was, I had to look down to catch myself on a stone lantern.

When I looked up again, I couldn't believe my eyes. Riley was crouched down, smiling and clucking. And Meow was strolling right up to him!

I gasped, half expecting the cat to come within arm's length only to dash away again. But no. A second later he was rubbing his pointy little head against Riley's knee.

Riley chuckled and scooped him up. "Good boy," he cooed as the cat started bumping his head against his chin. "There you go."

I rushed over. "How'd you do that?" I exclaimed.

"Animals like me, I guess," Riley said with a smile, cradling Meow like a baby as the cat purred loudly. "Now come on, let's get him inside before he makes another break for it."

I followed him into the house, feeling limp with relief as I shut the door firmly behind us. "Thanks for catching him," I said as we wandered into the living room. "My whole family would be devastated if anything happened to that crazy cat. I don't know what I would have done if you weren't here."

"Well, if I wasn't here, then he probably wouldn't have escaped in the first place. But you're welcome." Riley tried to deposit Meow onto the back of the couch. But in one of his patented moves, the cat sort of flipped himself over and clung to Riley's shirt with his front claws.

I laughed. "I think he likes you."

Riley grinned, giving up on setting the cat down. Instead he sank onto the couch and started rubbing Meow's head, causing the cat to purr like a miniature freight train.

"I like cats," Riley said. "We can't have one, 'cause my little sister's allergic. But I play with Marcus's stepmom's cats all the time."

I perched on the arm of the sofa, watching him run his hands over Meow's head and neck as the cat arched his back blissfully. My panic was subsiding. And being replaced by a question. What was Riley doing here?

"Um . . . so you said you wanted to talk," I said when I couldn't stand the suspense any longer.

He looked up at me. His smile faded, and I was pretty sure I saw him swallow hard.

"Oh, right," he said. "I did."

"So what do you want to talk about?" I wasn't planning on making this easy for him. Why should I? Just because those pings were starting up again, it didn't mean I should totally give up all my dignity and self-respect.

He glanced down at the cat again before returning his gaze to me. "Look, I really think you're cool," he said, his voice low and uncertain. "That's why I'm here. I feel like we went a little wrong last night, and you know, I just don't want that to happen if I can help it. But the thing is, all the Planetarium Girl stuff . . ." He paused and rubbed his face with the hand that wasn't stroking Meow. "I guess what I'm saying is I just want to stay friends for now. I hope you understand."

"Not really," I said before I could stop myself. Then I shrugged. Why *should* I stop myself from saying it? It was the truth.

He looked more uncomfortable than ever. "I don't really understand it either," he said. "I've never had anything like this happen before."

"You mean meeting someone at the planetarium and searching all over Maryland for her?" It came out a little more sarcastic than I'd intended, but he didn't seem to notice.

"No. I mean the whole love at first sight thing." One corner of his mouth twisted up into a rueful half smile. "Or not even sight, really, since I didn't get much of a look at her. But you know what I mean." He glanced down just long enough to tickle Meow under the chin. "Usually, I'm not so much into the big romantic gestures or whatever. I like to get to know a girl first, hang out with her, see how we get along, that kind of thing."

"Yeah," I said, almost more to myself than to him. "Me too."

"But this time . . ." He shook his head, a range of emotions playing out over his face. "I don't know. It was different. I met that girl at the planetarium, and I couldn't stop thinking about her, and then I came home and wrote the best song I'd ever written because of her. That has to mean something, right?" He shrugged. "So I just really need to give things a chance to play out there, see if that girl and I really are meant for each other."

It was all I could do to stop myself from jumping up and shouting, *Duh! I'm that girl!*

But I managed to just sit there and smile blandly. Why couldn't he see the truth that was sitting right there in front of him? That *I* was the one and only Planetarium Girl? I didn't get it. Was it the hair thing? Maybe if I tied my hair back right now, showed him how it looked when it was off my face . . .

But no. It was too late for that. What would be the point? He'd already decided that I wasn't The One.

Sixteen

"So how did he look when he said he just wanted to be friends?" Britt asked.

"I already told you ten times. He looked like he always looks."

"You mean devastatingly handsome?"

I shot her an irritated glance. "You're not helping," I informed her.

The two of us were on our way home from school the next day. Britt was driving.

She stopped at a red light and glanced over at me. "All I know is, a guy who 'just wants to be friends' doesn't usually show up on your doorstep like that. Pretty romantic, really."

"Thanks, Madame Romance."

"It's true," she insisted. "When was the

last time any of your other guy friends came rushing over to see if you were okay just because you got annoyed with him?"

The light changed. I waited until Britt had made it safely through the intersection before I spoke again. She can be a little distractible. "Okay, so maybe you have a point in a way," I admitted once we were safely cruising down the street. "I mean, he *did* feel those sparks when we first met, right?"

"Totally! Why else would he go searching for you on Facebook? Even if he doesn't know it's you." She paused for a second, clearly thinking through that sentence to make sure it made sense. "Anyway, it's obvious he likes you—you just need to figure out why he doesn't want to admit it."

"Or maybe not," I countered. "Maybe this whole situation is working out fine."

She shot me a suspicious look. "What do you mean?"

"I mean, if I can just wait out Riley's obsession with finding *her*—"

"Oh, the irony!" Britt put in, rolling her eyes.

"Exactly. But anyway, if I can wait that out and just be friends with him in the meantime, maybe he'll come around on his own.

You know—realize I'm right there under his nose, Planetarium Girl or not. In fact, maybe that would be better. For both of us."

Britt still looked dubious. "So that's your plan?" she said. "Just wait him out and eventually fall into the friends with benefits thing like you always do?"

"Hey, it's worked for me before." I shrugged. "And this time I have a head start. I already know he's looking for love. Like you said, he just hasn't figured out right now that he's looking for it with *me*."

That was the conclusion I'd reached yesterday after Riley had gone home. His little speech had actually helped me see the light. It wasn't that he wasn't interested in me; he'd all but admitted that he was. At least if you read between the lines a little.

No, it was just that no matter how much he might like me, he liked the idea of Planetarium Girl even more. His friends said he was stubborn once he got an idea in his head, and this proved it. He wasn't willing to give up on finding his muse, the mysterious girl from the museum. And whether it was the hair or something else, he'd already convinced himself that *she* wasn't *me*.

Britt turned down a side street. "Okay, waiting around and stuff is one idea," she said. "But how about this instead? We could figure out a way to get him somewhere dark—maybe a movie theater or whatever. Then you go and fling yourself at him again and see if he catches on."

"Um, that would be a no."

"Come on! You won't even consider it?" At my look, she shrugged. "Okay, then how about this? We invite him over to my house to hang out with us and some friends and, you know, listen to that crazy band you both like or something. At an opportune moment, everyone else can leave so you two are alone, just as a nice, slow song comes on. . . ."

This time I just sighed. "Listen, Britt, I don't think you can force a Moment to happen like that. I'm not sure it works that way. At least not for me," I added quickly before she could argue back with any of her own romantic conquests.

But she didn't even try. "Yeah, maybe you're right," she said thoughtfully, tapping her fingers on the steering wheel. "You're not really a Moment kind of girl."

"Hey!" I couldn't help being vaguely insulted. But then I shrugged it off. After all, she was right. "Yeah, it's true. But that's okay. I've always had the best luck with guys by being friends for a while first. So why should things be different with Riley just because we met in a weirder way?"

"I guess." She sounded dubious.

But I was starting to feel more certain than ever that I was on the right track. I was doing what was familiar and comfortable. There was something to be said for that, right?

I settled back against the car seat. "Anyway, I'm not too worried about waiting," I said. "After all, it's not like Riley is ever going to find Planetarium Girl anywhere else but right here."

★

What r u doing?

I pushed aside my Spanish book and leaned over the laptop to answer Riley's message. It was Wednesday afternoon, and I was cramming for that test. But there was always time for a little Facebook break.

Wishing I spent half my life living in other countries like u did. Maybe then I wouldn't b so worried about flunking my Spanish test mañana.

I sent the message, smiling at the thought of how he'd probably chuckle when he read it. Then I turned back to my studying.

Things had been going pretty well since my epiphany after Riley's visit. I could tell that Britt still wasn't too impressed by my plan—such as it was—but I wasn't too concerned about that. I was at peace with it.

Riley and I had fallen into a regular correspondence through Facebook and texting. Even though we weren't communicating face to face, I felt as if I was getting to know him better every day. We had a ton of stuff in common and never ran out of things to say to each other. It didn't hurt that our senses of humor meshed just as perfectly as our taste in music.

In other words, we were becoming friends. I was trying to remind myself not to look for anything more than that right now. It was all part of the process.

It wasn't always easy to remember that,

though. For instance, Riley had invited me and Britt to come see his band, the Grovers, play at a local coffeehouse that Friday night. And every time I thought about seeing him again in person, the pinging started up in my head and I couldn't help flashing back to that mind-blowing moment when we were dancing at the party. . . .

But I always did my best to push that sort of thought aside. I just had to be patient and let the process play out.

"Oh God." Britt rolled her eyes as my laptop buzzed. "What's Mr. Wonderful want this time?"

I just grinned at her and rolled over to grab the laptop off the rug by her bed. It was Thursday after school, and now that my Spanish test was over, Britt and I were in her room working on the English papers that were due the following week. With all my mooning over Riley lately, I'd fallen behind on homework, and now I was trying to catch up. As for Britt, well, she's almost *always* behind on her homework.

Sure enough, there was another message from Riley waiting for me. My smile faded a bit as I read it.

"What's wrong?" Britt asked, watching me.

I shrugged. "Nothing, really. I'm just wondering if Riley and I are getting a little *too* friends-only, you know? I mean, it's kind of cool that he's starting to confide in me about the ongoing quest for his planetarium princess. But . . ."

"You don't want to think about him checking out other girls." Britt nodded. "I hear ya. Friends is one thing. You don't want to take it too far and become one of the guys."

"Yeah." Over the past day or two Riley and I had started to joke around a little about the whole Planetarium Girl thing. That had been one thing. A good sign, really, at least up to a point. But somehow it had quickly turned into him updating me on how his search was going.

I scanned the message again. This time it seemed Riley had made contact with a new Facebook friend that he hoped might pan out. For some reason he seemed to find meaning in the fact that she hadn't written to him until now, well over a week after that fateful meeting in the planetarium.

It all made me feel a little queasy. But I did my best not to worry about it. In fact I tried to look on the bright side. At least this way I could keep track of how soon he might give up on this impossible quest of his.

On Friday afternoon Britt dropped me off at home right after school. "Sure you don't want me to consult on your outfit for tonight?" I asked her as I climbed out of her car at the curb. "Marcus will be there, remember?"

She shook her head. "I'll be fine. I'm the one playing wingman tonight, remember? You need to focus on *your* outfit. I want you to look so luscious that Riley will forget all the words to his songs the instant he lays eyes on you."

I laughed. "We'll see. Even fashion has its limits."

As I hurried toward the door, I heard my laptop buzz inside my bag. But I ignored it for the moment, not wanting to start multitasking and possibly let Meow escape again. The cat seemed to have been encouraged by his recent outdoor adventure and was being even more obnoxious about trying to dash out any chance he got.

I made it safely inside, grabbing Meow with one hand while pushing the door shut behind me with the other. Then I headed for the stairs, mentally planning my outfit. I wanted to look good for Riley's band's performance, just in case tonight was the night he came to his senses.

It wasn't until I slung my backpack onto my bed that I remembered that buzz. I almost ignored it, figuring whatever it was could probably wait. Then I realized it might be Riley, and I unzipped the pack to pull out the laptop.

Sure enough, the message was from Riley. I clicked on it as I kicked off the shoes I'd worn to school, already trying to figuring out which ones would look the best with the outfit I had in mind for tonight. I was so distracted that it took a moment to register what I was reading.

Hey L, this is so huge, u'll never believe it, but it's true.

** I found her! **

I'm sure of it this time. I finally found Planetarium Girl!!!!!!!

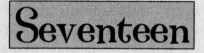

Seventeen

I froze in horror, wondering if my eyes were playing tricks on me. But no matter how many times I blinked, the words on the screen didn't change.

Sinking down onto the edge of my bed, I tried to take this in, to figure out what was happening. He sounded so certain he'd found the real Planetarium Girl at last. But how could he be so sure? Unless . . .

Could he be talking about me? I wondered with a flash of hope. Maybe he'd just figured it out, and this was his way of letting me know. It would be just like him to joke around like that. . . .

My heart pounding, I clicked through

onto his wall. As soon as I did, my heart plummeted into my toes.

Her name was Megan. She was a junior at East Elm and had almost as many FB friends as Britt did. Her hair was dark and short, with cute little wisps sticking out over her forehead and around her ears; her skin was pale and flawless. According to her "About Me" info section, which she'd left open to Friends of Friends, her favorite thing about herself was her green eyes, though in her photos they looked plain old hazel to me.

I gritted my teeth as I read her latest update: *Megan is . . . in luv already! Smooches, R!!! xoxoxo*

"Gross," I muttered as I scrolled down farther. There was a comment from Riley there saying how glad he was he'd finally found her. When I went back to his page, I saw that she'd made several entries on his wall as well, plus she'd sent him several goopy hearts-and-kisses type Superpokes.

When I reached out to scroll down farther, I realized my hand was shaking. This was so not what I'd been expecting tonight. How had it happened? How could he possibly think this perky twit was The One?

I grabbed the phone and dialed Britt.

When I told her the news, she let out a gasp so loud I probably could have heard it even without the phone.

"Oh! My! God!" she cried. "This is crazy. But don't worry, babe. He'll figure out that this one's as fake as all the others."

"I don't know." My gaze wandered back to the laptop screen. I winced as I saw a new message pop up. It was another cutesy comment to Riley from Megan. "This time seems different. He's acting kind of serious about it already."

"After like an hour, if that? Don't be ridiculous."

Despite my stomach-churning anxiety, I couldn't help smiling. Britt was the last person who should be criticizing anyone else for moving fast when it came to romance! But I didn't bother to point that out.

"Whatever," I said instead. "Do you think we should forget about going to the show?"

"Of course not, you loon! Riley's a smart guy. He'll catch on soon enough. With any luck he'll be over her before the Grovers start warming up tonight."

Britt was wrong. Oh, so very, very wrong.

When we walked into the coffeehouse,

it was crowded with people our age. Among them was Megan. I recognized her instantly. And not just because I'd seen her photos. She was hanging on Riley's arm like an over-sized purse. As I watched, he turned to say something to her. She stood on tiptoes and planted a kiss on his chin, making him smile and blush a little.

My heart sank. "So much for being over her," I muttered to Britt.

"Yeah." She sounded subdued. "But don't panic yet, babe."

The coffeehouse was a long, narrow place with exposed copper piping along the ceiling and a brick wall behind the counter. Several baristas were doing a booming business hand-ing out lattes and cappuccinos as fast as their gleaming machines could make them. At the far end of the place was a small wooden stage; tattered concert posters for old-school bands like the Kinks, Steppenwolf, and the Grateful Dead covered the walls around it like wallpaper. The sounds of foaming milk harmonized with the spittle of feedback from the amps and the lazy staccato tapping of a guy sitting behind a drum kit at the back of the stage. Everything smelled like—what else?—coffee.

Riley was leaning against the counter about halfway back toward the stage. He hadn't noticed us yet. As I stared at him, he turned to speak to a guy holding a guitar—presumably one of his bandmates. When the guy wandered off, Riley turned and finally spotted me.

My heart sank. If his face had been a text message, it would have said only one thing: *OOPS!*

"I'm guessing he already forgot he invited us," I whispered to Britt.

Riley said something to Megan, then came toward us. Megan stayed right with him, looking me and Britt over with critical eyes.

"Hi," Riley said when he reached us. "I'm glad you guys could make it. Um, this is Megan. Megan, this is Britt, and, um, Lauren. They're friends of mine."

"Nice to meet you," Megan said. Her voice matched her look—cute and perky. "I can't wait to meet all of Riley's friends."

Someone near the back of the room shouted Riley's name. He glanced that way.

"Sorry, gotta go get ready," he said, sounding relieved. "Enjoy the show, guys."

"Break a leg, baby!" Megan sang out as he rushed off.

That left her standing with us. Britt was staring at her. Uh-oh.

"So, Megan," she said in a casual voice. *Too* casual. "How'd you and Riley meet?"

Megan's giggle bubbled out of her like frothy foam from the cappuccino machine. "Well, first we met at the planetarium, of course," she said. "But after that I thought I'd never see him again. Then a friend of mine saw his adorable post on Facebook and the rest is history!"

She gave a cute little toss of her head that looked like a patented move. Britt can spot one of those a mile away, and no wonder. She's got a bunch of them herself. Her eyes narrowed.

"Really," she said, drawing out the *r* for effect. "So you're still claiming to be Planetarium Girl, huh?"

"I'm not *claiming* anything." Megan smoothed down the tendrils of hair around her perky little ears. Her earrings were silver dropped hearts that looked like real Gucci. "I *am* Planetarium Girl. Just ask Riley."

"Ooo-kay." Britt did nothing to hide her skepticism. "Far be it from me to criticize another girl's methods or whatever. But what are you after? I mean, are you really into Riley or are you just having fun?"

"What's it to you?" Dropping her hand from her hair, Megan looked Britt up and down. "Wait, let me guess—you made a play for him yourself, but he shot you down. Sorry, sweetie, guess you're just not his type."

She smiled smugly. Britt looked outraged. "Are you kidding me?" she exclaimed. "*I'm* not Planetarium Girl, and unlike you, I'm not pathetic and desperate enough to start pretending I am. But if you want to know the *truth* about this whole Planetarium Girl fiasco, I can—"

"Hey, I could really use some caffeine!" I said loudly, grabbing her and yanking her off balance. She was so surprised that she stopped yelling for a second. "Come on, Britt," I said, shooting her a meaningful look. "Let's go get an espresso or something, okay?"

For a second I didn't think it was going to work. She kept glaring at Megan, who continued to look smug. And perky.

I didn't give up. This whole evening was turning into a huge disaster as it was. The last thing I wanted to add to it was an embarrassing scene.

Finally Britt glanced at me, and that seemed to clue her in to how upset I was.

She allowed me to drag her off a few yards. I'm not sure Megan even noticed. She'd just reached into her purse for a compact and was checking her makeup.

I turned away, not wanting to see any more of her. "Come on," I told Britt in a low voice that I tried really, really hard to keep from shaking. "I think maybe we should just get out of here."

"Sure. Come on, I'll buy you a milkshake or something on the way home. No sense wasting these outfits, right?"

"Hey, look who's here!" a familiar voice sang out as we turned toward the door.

Marcus came bounding into the place. Rachel and a few other friends were right behind him.

Beside me I heard Britt let out a little gasp. Out of the corner of my eye I could see her do a quick hair check and wet her lips.

For a second, surprise chased away my misery. I'd almost forgotten about the boy-fight incident at that party. Afterward Britt had told me she'd decided to make out with Marcus because she was tired of Tommo and wanted an easy way to chase him off. But maybe there was more to it than that. Could she really be attracted to him?

"Actually, maybe we should stay after all," I told her in a low voice.

"What? No," she said, her eyes flickering from Marcus to me and then back again. "Um, I mean, I know you want to leave, so . . ."

"It's okay," I assured her. "We can stay for a little while if you want to hang out with Marcus."

By then he'd reached us, so I couldn't say anything more. He grabbed me in a bear hug, then turned to Britt and hugged her, too. "Hey," he told her. "I got that video you sent me. Pretty funny!"

I shot her a surprised look. She carefully avoided my eye, staying focused on Marcus. "Awesome," she said. "I figured you might get a kick out of it."

It sounded as if Britt and Marcus had stayed in touch since meeting at the party last weekend. So why was this the first I was hearing about it?

No big shock there, I told myself. *I've been more than a little self-absorbed this week. She probably did mention it, but I was too busy mooning over Unavailable Boy to pay attention.*

Rachel and Haley came over and said hi. "Glad you came, Lauren," Rachel told me. "You'll love the Grovers—they're really good."

"Yeah." Haley grinned and tossed her friend a look. "And not in that we-have-to-like-it-cause-they're-our-friends kind of way, either. They're actually, like, *good* good."

"I can't wait to hear them." That was both true and not. On the one hand I'd been dying to see what Riley's band could do since the first time he'd mentioned he was in one. Somehow, though, I wasn't really in the mood at the moment. . . .

"So did you hear?" Rachel asked me. "Riley found another Planetarium Girl."

"Yeah. I heard," I said.

Haley grimaced. "I checked her out on Facebook. This one seems even more shallow and annoying than the last one."

"Really? I didn't think that was possible." Rachel stood on her tiptoes, peering at the crowd near the stage. "Where is she, anyway? Have you seen her, Lauren?"

"Uh-huh. She's over there. The dark-haired girl in last year's Juicy cami." I pointed to Megan, who was watching Riley tune his bass as if it were the most fascinating thing she'd ever seen.

Rachel grinned, shooting Haley a mischievous look. "Should we go say hi?"

"Oh, yes. I do so enjoy chatting with

Riley's new little friends." Haley looked equally amused. "Coming?" she asked me.

"You guys go ahead. I, uh, want to grab a drink before the show starts."

They hurried off toward Megan. I made my way over to the counter and ordered myself an iced coffee. Then I looked around for Britt. She was across the way, leaning back against the wall and smiling up at Marcus, who was doing the one-arm casual lean thing over her.

Okay. Looked like she was still busy. I could see Rachel and Haley chatting up Megan, who looked bored and a little annoyed. But I hung back, doing my best to find a spot where I could see the stage but Riley couldn't see me.

Unfortunately, seeing the stage also meant seeing Megan. I stared moodily at her. It was bad enough that Riley had found someone else. At least if it had been someone cool, like Rachel or Haley or whoever, I maybe could have accepted it and just been happy being his friend.

But Megan wasn't cool. She was pretty much the *opposite* of cool. That made her definitely not good enough for him. So why couldn't he see that? Was he really so caught up in his silly fantasy about his Planetarium Girl muse that he would hook up with anyone who could convince him that she was her?

I was still stewing over that when a sudden explosion of bass made the whole place jump, including me. A second later the rest of the band joined in. The show was on.

Despite everything I found myself nodding along to the music. Riley's friends had been right. The band *was* good. They weren't really that similar in sound to the Beast, which surprised me a little. But maybe it shouldn't have. It was clear that Riley was open to a lot of things—he'd had to be, living in so many places during his childhood. Why should his musical tastes be any different? Besides, I liked a lot of different music too. Just one more thing the two of us had in common. . . .

After a while I hardly even noticed Megan grooving sexily away at the edge of the stage anymore. Okay, that's a lie. I noticed. But I was trying really hard not to care so much.

Maybe Riley and I really were meant to be just friends. And maybe that was okay. I should have known better than to fall so hard for him—and for the idea of love at first sight.

The current song ended. "And now we've got something kind of special," the lead singer said into the microphone. "Riley, come on up here, bro."

Riley set down his bass and stepped forward, taking the mic from his bandmate. He looked eager, confident, and a little shy all at the same time.

"Hey," he said to the audience. "Thanks for coming out tonight. Hope you all don't mind, but I wrote a new song recently and I wanted to debut it tonight. Anyone who's been checking out Facebook lately probably knows the one I mean."

There was a scattering of laughter and applause. Someone—I was pretty sure it was Marcus—let out a loud whoop.

Riley cleared his throat. "Okay, then, here goes. It's called 'We Should Stop Meeting Like This.'"

He glanced back at the rest of the band and counted them off. They started playing, and a moment later Riley started to sing.

It was a love song, mostly. But it was

also all about luck, being in the right place at the right time, and paying attention to fate. Riley's voice didn't really have the grit and power of the other singer, but it was full of sincerity and meaning. It was obvious that he really believed in what he was singing.

I closed my eyes, just letting the raw emotion of the song wash over me. Every time he hit a high note, I felt myself shiver. The song was amazing. Just . . . amazing.

It ended with a flourish of cymbals, and I smiled. A tiny homage to MTIAB and "Squid for Breakfast," perhaps? Opening my eyes, I was just in time to see Riley hurry forward to the edge of the stage.

Megan was waiting for him there. She tilted her head up as he bent down and kissed her. There was a chorus of "Awww!" from the audience as the happy couple clung together, joined at the lips for a long, lingering moment. Before long someone—again, probably Marcus—shouted, "Get a room!"

As for me, I didn't make a peep. All I could do was stand there, my smile frozen on my face as reality came crashing down around me. No matter how much I'd been trying to convince myself that I didn't care, I still did. That was supposed to be *my* song, *my* kiss . . . my guy. But it wasn't. *He* wasn't. Not really, not anymore.

And that was so *not* fair. . . .

Eighteen

"I'm really not in the mood for shopping," I complained as Britt and I walked into the mall the next day.

"Really? Wow, I guess there really is a first time for everything." She gave me a searching look, as if gauging my exact mood by my reaction to the jibe. "Seriously, though. We need to take your mind off things. You always say you're not the wallowing type, right?"

I shrugged. She had a point. Maybe shopping would be just the thing to take my mind off my near-miss at love at first sight. Not that I believed in that. . . .

It was still hard to accept that things had ended the way they had. But there it was.

No doubt about it. The image of Riley and Megan kissing was seared into my retinas; it was all I saw when I closed my eyes.

The mall was packed, which was no surprise on a Saturday. Gangs of shoppers prowled in and out of stores or wandered down the broad center aisle. Britt and I slipped into this river of humanity, drifting past one brightly colored store display after another.

Britt checked her watch. "Where do you want to go first?" she asked.

I shrugged. Normally, I'm all about shopping. I don't buy that many of my clothes at the mall, preferring to be a little more creative in my fashion stylings. But it's always fun to look around, keep up on the trends, get ideas for my own designs, and maybe pick up some cool accessories or whatever.

Today, however, my heart just wasn't in it. "Wherever you want," I said. "I'm not really looking for anything."

"Mind if we stop at the food court, then?" Britt asked. "I could use a soda."

"Sure."

We headed up the escalator. Soon we were surrounded by the scents of grease and baking cookies. It was a little early for the lunch rush, so the food court wasn't very crowded. That made it easy to hear a familiar shout coming from over near the cookie place. Looking that way, I saw Marcus dancing around balancing a straw on his nose. I also saw the usual group of friends watching him and laughing. Including Riley.

"Oh, look," Britt said. "It's Marcus and the gang."

I shot her a suspicious look. "Did you know they were going to be here?" I hissed.

Her return look oozed guilt. "Um, not exactly. Well, Marcus did mention that they were thinking of meeting up here around now. . . ."

There was no time to strangle her. Marcus had just dropped his straw, looked around, and spotted us.

"Check it out!" he cried, sounding as happy as if he's just discovered a pot of gold right there in front of Cookie and Co. "It's our favorite pair of Potomac pretties."

"Hey, guys," Rachel called out in her usual friendly way as Britt and I approached. Haley, Jake, one of the video-game-playing girls from the party, and another guy whose name I didn't remember added their greetings.

Riley said hi too. At least I assumed he

did. I was too busy having a nervous break-down to know for sure. As soon as we were out of here, I was definitely going to kill Britt. All I had to figure out was how pain-ful to make it and where to hide the body.

"So Riley," Britt said in a slightly-too-bright voice. "Where's your new squeeze? I thought you two were pretty much joined at the hip these days."

"You mean Megan?" Riley shrugged. "She's in DC for the weekend, visiting her sister who goes to GWU."

I felt my shoulders, which had gone tense at the sight of him, relax a little. At least I wouldn't have to watch the happy couple smooching or holding hands today. At least there was that.

The next few minutes passed in a daze. Somehow I found myself wandering down the mall holding an orange soda. And I don't even like orange soda. As the others hurried forward toward the music and mov-ies store, Riley fell into step beside me.

"Hey," he said, touching me briefly on the arm.

"Hey." I tried to ignore the way my arm had suddenly started tingling.

"So I looked for you after the show

last night." He shot me a sidelong look. "Wanted to hear what you thought of the band. Guess you'd already left, though."

"Yeah, I had to get home. But you guys were great. Practically Beastworthy."

He grinned. "Thanks. I know that's a serious compliment coming from you."

"Totally." I smiled back. "Um, so did Megan like the show?"

Yeah, I couldn't resist. Same way I can never resist probing with my tongue right after having a tooth pulled, or peeling off a scab, or peeking at the gory scenes in a movie even after I've covered my eyes.

His expression went a little gooey around the edges. "She loved it," he said. "And listen, Lauren, I want to thank you for listening this whole time, you know? It's good to have friends who, like, support what you really want."

"Um . . ." I wasn't sure what to say to that.

Luckily, he wasn't paying that much attention. "Anyway, get this—Megan and I made plans to meet up at the Air and Space Museum tomorrow at noon. Isn't that, you know, super-romantic?"

"Definitely romantic." It was so difficult

to spit out the words that I was astounded by how normal they sounded.

Not that Riley would have noticed either way. His eyes were a million miles away. Well, probably more like fifteen or twenty miles away, in the city—with Megan.

"Back to the place where we first met," he mused. Then he snapped back to the here and now, reaching into his pocket and pulling something out. "That's when I'm going to show how much it means to me that I found her again by giving her this. Check it out—think she'll like it?"

He dangled the item in front of me. I grabbed it for a better look. It was a guitar pick on a thin silver chain.

"That's the pick I used at my very first real gig with the Grovers," he explained shyly. "I kept it as a souvenir or whatever. Kind of dumb, huh? But I thought it might be a nice way to let her know how happy I am that we found each other, you know?"

I gulped, staring at the pick. It had a couple of nicks in it and looked pretty ordinary overall. But that didn't matter. I could tell by the way he was talking that it was superspecial to him. That this—the necklace, the meeting at the museum—was going to be his way of letting Megan know that he wanted to take things to the next level in their relationship.

It was an incredibly touching and romantic plan. Or at least it would have been if that annoying faker Megan weren't so utterly and completely undeserving of such a sweet, earnest gesture.

"Sounds cool." I tried to keep my voice casual and disinterested as I handed back the necklace. Because if I let myself tell him what I really thought, I was pretty sure I was going to burst into tears right there in the middle of the mall.

He looked a little surprised by my reaction, or nonreaction, or whatever. But he didn't say a word as he tucked the guitar pick back into his pocket. We just stood there for a moment in silence, neither of us looking at the other, though out of the corner of my eye I could see him hazarding a glance or two my way.

When I couldn't stand it anymore, I forced a laugh. It came out sounding fake and kind of mean. "Well, are we just going to stand around here all day, or are we going to shop?"

Without waiting for an answer, I hurried into the music store. Rachel and Haley were over near the registers looking at the rack of new releases, and I spotted Britt and Marcus giggling together over something in the kiddie section. Behind me I could hear Riley's footsteps. Not wanting to look at him right then, I stepped over to the nearest bin of CDs and started digging through them without really seeing them.

He came up beside me and stood there for a moment. I realized I was holding my breath. When I let it out and breathed in again, I caught a whiff of his distinctive spicy-soapy-coffee scent, the one I'd first noticed back at the planetarium. But I did my best to ignore the flutter it caused in my stomach.

"Are you okay?" he asked after a moment.

I didn't meet his eye, instead busying myself with the next row of CDs, flipping through them one at a time. "Sure, fine."

"Are you positive?" He leaned on the edge of the bin, trying to get a look at my face. "Because I never knew you were so into opera."

I blinked, finally focusing in on those

CDs. Oops. Dropping the one I'd just picked up, I shrugged and moved on.

"What's the big?" I said. "I have eclectic tastes; so sue me."

He frowned, watching me as I paused by the dancehall section. "Look," he said after a moment. "If you're mad at me or something, at least tell me what I did, okay?"

For a second I was tempted. Why not lay things on the line? *Somebody* had to tell Riley he was making a huge mistake before he made a complete fool of himself over a girl who didn't deserve him. . . .

But the feeling passed quickly. I'd already tried being honest. What was the point in trying again now that he was so sure he'd found her? If his longtime pals couldn't get through to him, what chance did I have? At least if I kept quiet, maybe we could still be friends. That was better than nothing, right? And I wasn't the type to pine away over someone who was into someone else. No way. I definitely wasn't *that* pathetic. As Britt was always saying, there were plenty of fish in the sea.

"Sorry," I said, turning to face him. "Guess I'm just a little distracted today.

Listen, about that necklace—I'm sure Megan will adore it. Any girl would."

"Really?" His face lit up. "Thanks, Lauren."

"You're welcome. And hey, good luck tomorrow, okay? I'm sure it'll be awesomely romantic."

He smiled, looking relieved. "Thanks," he said again. "You're the best. Did I mention I'm glad we met?"

"Yeah. But it's always nice to hear it." I smiled at him, feeling my heart break a little. But I did my best to ignore it. Not pathetic—nope, not me.

Once I'd convinced Riley that I was happy for him, I almost managed to convince myself, too. Or at least forget everything that had happened and try to have a good time.

And before long I actually was—having a good time, that is. Riley and his friends were a blast. Marcus kept us all in stitches with his lively sense of humor; a few times Britt laughed so hard I was afraid she was going to pass out.

I couldn't help noticing that Britt wasn't acting quite like herself. At least not when it came to Marcus. I first noticed when he stepped aside to let her go first on the escalator. Instead of saying something obnoxious, she just thanked him and went ahead.

A little after that we stopped in the candle store so Haley could buy a present for her aunt's birthday. Britt found a juniper-scented candle that she liked. And when Marcus joked about buying it for her for Christmas, she didn't say something Britt-like, like, "Why wait? Christmas is a long time from now," or, "Hey, if you're offering, I could use a new Coach bag." Instead she just smiled at him and held out the candle for him to smell too. The light was kind of dim in there—candles, remember?—but I almost would have sworn that she blushed a little. Almost. Because Britt *does not* blush.

And when we were all browsing in Macy's and she held up a purple top for his opinion, she actually listened when he said he liked the blue one for her better . . . and grabbed the blue one!

"Think I'll try it on," she said.

"I'll come with you." I grabbed the first thing I could find that was anywhere near my size—a boring beige polo—and followed her into the dressing room. As soon as we were alone in one of the roomy stalls, I tossed the polo aside. "So what's going on with you and Marcus?" I demanded.

She pulled her T-shirt off over her head. "What do you mean?" she asked, her voice muffled by the fabric.

I waited until I could see her face again before answering. "I mean you're acting different with him," I said. "You're not treating him like your usual boy toys. If I didn't know better, I'd swear you actually, you know, liked and respected him."

Britt grabbed the blue top. "So what? I like and respect all my boy toys."

"Yeah, for like twelve and a half seconds." I crossed my arms, leaned back against the dressing room's full-length mirror, and stared at her. "But it's been a whole entire week now and you're not acting sick of him yet."

She yanked on the top and adjusted it. "Move over; I can't see myself." As soon as I shifted out of the way, she twisted and turned in front of the mirror. "He was right," she murmured. "The blue one's definitely better."

"Aha! See?" I pointed an accusatory

finger in her face. "Since when do you ever listen to guys for fashion advice!"

"I listen to Vivi's brother Austin all the time. He has great taste."

"I mean *straight* guys. Guys you're actually *dating*."

She didn't answer for a moment, keeping her head down and playing with the hem of the blue top. Finally she looked up and met my gaze. The look in her eyes was almost . . . bashful?

"Okay, maybe you're right," she said softly. "I think I might actually be, you know, falling for this one. For real, I mean." A little smile played around the corners of her mouth. "I'm even starting to wonder why I wasted my time with all those other losers."

My jaw dropped. Literally. I stood there with my mouth hanging open, staring at my best friend. Who was suddenly acting like some complete stranger.

"For real?" I demanded, once I'd recovered enough to speak. "You're actually doubting your man-eating ways?"

"Well, not *doubting*, exactly." She squared her shoulders and gazed at herself in the mirror. "Come to think of it, it was probably fate that things happened this way. If I hadn't kissed so many frogs, I might not have recognized a prince when I found him."

I was stunned. It was hard to believe that this could really be Britt talking about finding her prince—and maybe actually meaning it. But she had a look in her eye I'd never seen there before, especially when she looked at Marcus. Or mentioned his name. Or thought about him. Like she was obviously doing right now as she smiled at herself in the mirror.

"Wow," was all I could say for a second. Then I shook my head. "I'm thrilled for you, Britt. Seriously. At least this whole Planetarium Girl disaster turned out to be good for something."

"I know, right?" she said. "But it still blows my mind that Riley can't see that you guys are just as perfect for each other as Marcus and I are."

"Never mind that." I grabbed the polo, which I'd never had any intention of trying on. Boring Beige Blah just isn't my look. "Let's get out there so you can hang with your prince."

"Anyone want to split a pie?" Marcus asked, stopping in front of the pizza place. It was an hour later, and we were all starving.

"Sure," Britt said.

"Me too," Jake agreed.

Rachel nodded. "Let's get the large."

The others seemed ready to join in the pizza fest, too. But Riley and I exchanged a look.

"I'll pass," I said. "I'm in the mood for something a little more interesting than tomato sauce and processed cheese on undercooked dough."

Riley chuckled. "Ditto. Come on, Lauren. The Japanese place here isn't too bad. We'll find you guys in a minute, okay?"

I saw Britt shoot me a raised eyebrow, but I ignored it. This wasn't about romance. It was merely a matter of discernment. Riley and I left the others arguing the merits of pepperoni versus mushrooms and headed across the food court.

"It's nice to have someone along who likes to eat something more adventurous than pizza and burgers," Riley said as we got in line at the Japanese place, which really did have a fairly extensive menu for a mall place.

"Yeah," I agreed. "Most of my friends make a point to never eat anything more exotic than brown mustard. Britt definitely included. In fact, I'm pretty sure I'm a shoo-in for the title of Weirdest Eater in Maryland."

"Don't be so sure," he said jokingly. "I lived in Brazil, remember? They put peas and mashed potatoes on their hot dogs there."

"Kid stuff," I countered. "Last month my dad decided to make his own haggis. With all the traditional ingredients."

He nodded slowly, the expression on his face convincing me that he must have tried the disgusting Scottish dish himself at some point in his life. "Impressive," he said. "But have you ever tried stewed oxtail?"

"No," I had to admit. "But I'm sure if I mention it, my parents will declare next week Jamaican food week and give it a try."

He was still laughing when his phone buzzed. "Sorry," he said, reaching into his pocket. When he glanced down at it, he smiled. "Oh. Megan just texted me."

"That's nice." I carefully kept my voice and face neutral. Even though my good mood had just crashed and burned like the Hindenburg.

He was still reading the text. "She just wants to confirm our plans for tomorrow—

she's getting ready to hit the town with her sister."

We were almost to the front of the line by now, standing side by side. I was trying not to glance over and read the text for myself. Trying *really* hard.

But what can I say? I am weak. My eyes edged over in that direction, and before I could stop myself, I was scanning the message. It was pretty much what Riley had said, except that he'd left out one part. The part where she said, *Luv ya and miss ya, sweetie!* at the end.

Suddenly the smells of fish and soy sauce, which had made my stomach grumble hungrily just seconds ago, started making me feel nauseated instead. Or maybe it was the terrible truth that was turning my stomach. Because as I stood there beside Riley watching him read that text from his new girlfriend, I realized something.

I couldn't talk myself out of it. I didn't want to be "just friends" with Riley. No, I really, really, really liked this guy. And I was pretty sure he could have liked me back. But I'd totally blown my chance. And there was nothing I could do about it now.

It was too late.

Nineteen

I was still thinking about Britt's outfit when I headed up my front steps that evening. That is, the outfit I'd helped her pick out after our trip to the mall. For her date. With Marcus.

That's right. The two of them had plans to catch a movie and a late dinner that night. Britt was so giddy about their first real date that she'd barely been able to think about what to wear. Luckily, I was there to step in and make sure she looked amazing in her favorite little black dress from Anthropologie and some cool sparkly high-heeled Mary Janes I'd found her at a thrift store recently.

As I opened the door, I sniffed the air,

wondering what exotic epicurean delight was in store for me that evening. After all, it looked like I was going to be home for date night this weekend. I might as well know what I was getting myself into.

To my surprise all I smelled was cat food and dust. Chairman Meow was waiting to greet me by trying to dash outside as usual, but there was no sign of my parents bustling around the kitchen or setting up board games in the den. Slinging Meow over my shoulder, I headed for the steps, wondering if they were still out shopping—I hadn't checked the garage for their cars when Britt had dropped me off.

"Anybody home?" I shouted upstairs.

"Coming!" my father's faint voice replied.

I shrugged, shifting Meow to my other shoulder as I wandered over to the hall table to see if there was any mail for me. He purred and kneaded my back with his paws.

"Ow!" I complained, detaching him and setting him down. "Feels like somebody needs his claws clipped again."

Yeah. It was shaping up to be a super-exciting Saturday night indeed. . . .

"Hello, hello. We were just wondering if you'd be home before we left," my dad said, hurrying down the steps adjusting his tie.

His tie? Hold on. Back up. It was Saturday. And Dad's number one rule in life was No Ties on the Weekend. Exceptions made only for weddings and funerals.

I stared at him. "Why are you so dressed up?"

He did a little twirl. "Do I look okay, oh fashion-expert daughter?"

"You look hot, oh fashion-impaired father," I replied, still not really understanding. "But why? Since when do you dress up for date night?"

"Since we decided to take your advice," my mother replied.

I'd been so busy staring at Dad that I hadn't even heard her coming. Now I did a double take. She looked even more incredible than he did. She was wearing a red knit dress that showed off her trim figure, along with some chunky-heeled black pumps I'd helped her pick out and the earrings I'd given her for Christmas a year or two ago.

"Ooh la la!" I said. "But where are you going?"

"Out." My father reached for my mother's hand as she reached the bottom step. "Dancing."

He twirled her. It was a little awkward, since she twisted her arm the wrong way and they had to let go and try again. But it was cute. Especially when they both giggled like a pair of middle schoolers heading off to their first school dance.

Meanwhile I was still confused. "Dancing?" I echoed. "You guys don't go dancing. What happened to date night?"

"Actually, it was your question last weekend that got us thinking," Dad said.

My mother nodded. "We love our usual routine. But we decided maybe once in a while it might be fun to try something different. So we're taking your advice and going out dancing tonight."

I was stunned. My advice? Was that what it had been? In any case, I never would have expected this of my parents. Then again, who could have guessed they'd look so snazzy all gussied up, either?

"Wow," was all I could say as I grabbed Meow before he could sink his claws into Mom's stockings.

After my parents left, I heated up some leftover couscous and carried it into the den to eat in front of the TV. I scrolled through the recorded programs on the DVR, but for some reason nothing appealed to me. I ended up leaving the TV tuned to the Weather Channel just for company.

"This is weird," I said to Meow, who was sitting on the arm of the couch staring intently at my food. "Usually it's me going out somewhere fun on Saturday night while Mom and Dad stay here."

I took a bite and chewed slowly, pondering that. First Britt, now my parents, even Riley with his seemingly hopeless quest for Planetarium Girl . . . it seemed everyone I knew was turning their lives—or at least their love lives—upside down. So what about me? Did I dare try to follow their lead?

I thought about how great it had felt hanging out with Riley yesterday. And then how terrible it had felt knowing I'd missed my chance to really give things a try with him.

Or had I? Suddenly a plan popped into my head, one worthy of Britt's nuttiest moments. I dropped my fork and thought about it, turning it over in my head. It was so crazy it just might work . . . or would it?

I supposed it didn't matter. It wasn't as if I'd have the guts to try. . . .

Just then I noticed my sketch pad lying on the chair where I'd left it that morning. It was open to a recent design, an awesome gown with totally daring cutouts in the bodice and a funky hemline. The kind of outfit that would look amazing strutting down the runway—at least in my own humble opinion—but that I'd never in a million years have the guts to wear myself.

Or would I? Maybe if I thought I could ever really be the fashion designer I was in my dreams, I needed to start proving I had it in me to put myself out there. And I wasn't thinking about wearing some cutting-edge prom dress to school. No, I had something completely different in mind.

The cat let out a soft yowl and stretched one paw toward my food. I just stared at him. Even Chairman Meow was willing to fling himself out into the wide world without a thought of how he was going to get home again. . . .

I smiled as I recalled Riley cradling the crazy cat in his arms after the last escape. And thinking of Riley, remembering him that way, made me realize I had to try. After all, if he could put himself out there to find me—or her, or whoever—I should at least be willing to risk a little embarrassment to meet him halfway.

I took a deep breath as I stared up at the imposing, blocky façade of the Air and Space Museum. It was the next day, just a few minutes before noon. I'd hopped on the Metro early and spent the extra time wandering around the Mall fighting my jangling nerves and wondering if I could really do this.

But now that I was here, I felt ready for whatever was about to happen. Or at least resigned to giving it my best shot and seeing what came of it. Entering the museum, I headed upstairs immediately.

Riley was leaning against the wall near the top of the escalator. He was looking at his watch, which allowed me to get pretty close before he noticed I was there.

When he finally did look up, his eyes widened in surprise. But I didn't give him a chance to speak. I had to spit this out before I lost my nerve.

"We really *have* to stop meeting like this."

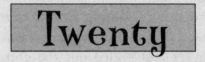

Twenty

"Wh-what are you doing here?" Riley blurted out, clearly startled. He took another look at his watch. "Megan will be here any minute."

"I know." I was slightly embarrassed to note that my voice was shaking. But I couldn't stop now. "I figured this was my last chance to let you know how I feel. Even if you don't believe I'm really the girl you met that day"—I waved a hand vaguely toward the planetarium—"well, I guess I wanted to do that much."

I gulped as he stared at me with panic in his eyes. "Wait," he said slowly. "What exactly are you trying to—"

"Sweetie!" Megan was breathless and giggling as she appeared at the top of the escalator, juggling her purse and her cell phone, and her eyes made a beeline for Riley. "Oh my God, I was afraid I was going to be late!"

Riley shot me an unreadable look. I held my breath, waiting for him to respond to what I'd said. But he just reached into his pocket and pulled out the guitar-pick necklace.

"Sorry." His voice sounded funny, as if it were coming from very far away. "I have to go."

Have you ever actually felt your heart breaking? I hope not. Because I'd never wish what I was feeling right then on anyone, not even my worst enemy. Not even Perky Megan.

I watched just long enough to see Riley hurry forward to meet Megan and bend down to kiss her. That was enough for me. She hadn't noticed me yet, and I wanted to keep it that way.

Sidling out of view behind a large informational sign, I looked for an escape route. All I wanted was to get back to the Metro, make my way home, and lock myself in my room for a good long cry. But a huge group of elementary school kids—maybe a Sunday school group? I didn't know, and didn't really care—had just started pouring up into the second-floor aisleway from the escalator. In my current condition I wasn't sure I could fight the screaming, laughing, shoving tide. So I just stood there, taking deep breaths and pressing my back against the wall to keep from passing out.

I'd tried. That was all I could do, right? Maybe if I kept telling myself that, I might actually start to feel better. Someday.

The young kids were making a lot of noise. But even so, I couldn't help overhearing Riley and Megan from the other side of the sign. I didn't want to—Lord knows I would have preferred to be anywhere else on the planet right then. Or even up in space in one of the rocket ships hanging from the vaulted ceiling. But I couldn't help it.

Riley started off by assuring Megan that she wasn't late. Megan just giggled and launched into some convoluted tale about how late she and her sister had stayed out the night before.

"It was, like, soooo much fun," she exclaimed. "I can't wait to ditch high school and get to college! You have sooo much more freedom and stuff."

"That's cool." Riley's voice was quieter, so much so that I could barely hear him. Even so I could tell that he sounded a little preoccupied. "But listen, Megan. I wanted to meet you here so I could give you something. It's, um, pretty special, just like you are to——"

"Hey!" Megan squawked, sounding irritated.

I couldn't resist a flash of curiosity. Sure, the guitar pick necklace didn't really go with Megan's girly, flirty fashion style. But it seemed impossible that she'd act so offended by just seeing it.

As it turned out, that wasn't what she was reacting to at all. Peeking around the edge of the sign, I saw her glaring at a couple of boys from the kiddie group. I guess they'd bumped into her or something.

"Why don't you watch where you're going?" she snapped at them.

"We were!" one of the little boys shot back.

"Yeah," his friend added. "We can't help it if you were staring around not paying attention."

They both stomped off. Riley laughed, sounding nervous. "Kids!" he said.

I ducked back behind the sign, checking around to see if the coast was clear. It wasn't. The kids seemed to be coalescing around the planetarium entrance.

"Anyway," Riley began. He was clearly unaware that I was still lurking around, listening like some psycho stalker, which made me feel guilty and a little helpless. "As I was saying—are you okay, Megan?"

"Hmm? Oh, sure." Megan giggled. "Sorry, just looking around."

There was such a long pause that I started to wonder with relief if they'd wandered out of earshot. But then Riley spoke again.

"Okay," he said, sounding uncertain. "It's just that you're staring at stuff like you've never seen this place before."

"What? Don't be silly, sweetie!" Her tinkling laugh cut through the elementary kids' chatter like a blade. "This is where we met, right? Right over there."

Again, a long pause. "Actually," Riley said. "The planetarium is that way."

"Oh, I know!" Megan said immediately. "I was talking about the first time I spotted you. Um, I was sitting right there, and my friend Caitlin says, 'Hey, check out the hottie—'"

"Are you sure about that?" Riley interrupted her. "Because I thought you said it was your friend Joanie who was with you."

"Joanie, Caitlin, whatever. As soon as I saw you, baby, I forgot all about everything else."

"Okay." Riley's voice sounded funny now. "Um, because right before you got here somebody was telling me something that made me wonder if you really are Planetarium Girl, and then you start acting like you're seeing this place for the first time . . ."

I froze, my body going hot and cold all at the same time. *Somebody?* Was he talking about me?

"What are you saying, baby?" For a second Megan sounded offended, or at least faux-fended. Then she laughed. "Okay, okay, you caught me. Whatever. I wasn't the chick in the planetarium. Actually, I didn't even go on that stupid field trip—I faked a cold so I could skip it. But when I saw that cute post of yours on Facebook, I just knew we'd be great together, especially since all the guys at my school are so lame and immature. . . ."

"Wait." Riley's voice sounded kind of

strangled. "So you—you're just another faker?"

"You don't have to be insulting about it." She sounded offended again now—this time for real. "I just wanted to meet you—you should be flattered. Anyway, what does it matter now that we're together? That reminds me. You said you had something for me, right?"

"Yeah, I did." Now his voice was steady. "But I'm thinking I made a mistake. Sorry, Megan. I wasn't trying to lead you on or anything, I swear. And I appreciate you taking time out from your sister to come and meet me here. I'm just not sure things are going to work out between us after all."

I froze. Was I imagining things, or was he . . . breaking up with her? My mind spun. What did this mean?

Just then one of the chaperones with the kids' group blew a whistle and yelled for all the kids to gather around. I scooted off to the side, trying to avoid getting caught up in the crush. In the meantime I missed a little of the conversation on the other side of the sign.

When I tuned in again, Megan was ranting at Riley, who wasn't saying much. "Oh yeah?" she fumed loudly. "Well, I guess I made a mistake too! Here I thought you were something special, and you're actually just another immature high school guy after all. I'm thinking I might as well just give up and go out with college guys. A whole bunch of them hit on me last night, you know. . . ."

There was more, I guess. But I didn't hear it. That was the good part. The bad part was that the reason I couldn't hear Megan anymore was that the kiddie group had just started charging into the planetarium. And I got swept in there right along with them.

"Excuse me!" I exclaimed, doing my best to fight the tide of twerps. "Please, I'm not supposed to be in here. . . ."

But it was no use. Finally, I gave up and just went along with it, figuring I could leave once the kids settled in their seats.

When I finally got myself turned around and aimed toward the door, I stopped short. Riley was standing there just inside the doorway!

Twenty-one

Judging by the expression on his face and the way he was holding up both arms and trying to dodge the short people who were surrounding him, I guessed he'd been caught up in the kiddie tsunami too.

Then he spotted me. His arms dropped to his sides and he just stared. Then he started fighting his way through the crowd—but in the opposite direction this time.

I waited, my heart pounding. Eventually he reached me.

"Hey," he said.

"Hey."

For a second we just stared at each other. I wasn't sure what to say. Finally the silence was too much for me.

"I heard what happened," I blurted out. "Just now. With you and Megan."

Yeah. Tactful, I know.

He grimaced. "You did?" he said. "Oh. Yeah. Guess you were right when you said she was just another faker."

Had I said that? I couldn't really remember.

"Sorry," I said, hating the pained look on his face.

"Don't be. It's my own stupid fault. I was so into the idea that I'd found her this time that I ignored my own doubts about her, not to mention some major signs. Like how much she and I *didn't* have in common, and—"

"Move it!" a little girl from the kiddie group ordered us, giving Riley a shove. "I'm supposed to be in this row!"

"Sorry." Riley stepped aside, letting her pass. Then he shot me a look. "Should we get out of here?"

I glanced at the doorway, which was still crowded with kids pouring in. "Yeah, good luck with that," I joked weakly.

"Hmm. Maybe you're right. Let's just get out of the way until things thin out." He led the way to a less-populated area near the front of the room.

Then I turned to face him again. I was starting to feel nervous. But I had to ask him the next question.

"So," I began tentatively. "About what you and I were talking about before she got here . . ."

His expression was troubled, and for a second I thought he was going to cut me off again. "Yeah," he said instead. "About that. The reason I was so freaked out about seeing you here—well, aside from the obvious . . ."

I chuckled self-consciously. "You mean having me randomly show up at another girl's big date?"

"Yeah, that." He smiled briefly, then went serious again. "But the main reason is because, well . . ." He took a deep breath. "It's because I've liked *you* all along."

"You—you have?" Somehow, this time I knew he wasn't talking about being just friends.

Riley nodded. "I mean, I never believed for a second that you were Planetarium Girl," he said with a smile. "One look at all this was enough to convince me of that."

He reached out and touched my hair. Okay, I know hair doesn't technically have nerve endings or anything. But even so, the touch made me shiver.

Then I came back to my senses, realizing what this meant. I opened my mouth to explain, to tell him about how I'd had my hair pulled back that day. My hands even twitched, getting ready to demonstrate.

But then I stopped myself. What difference did it make, anyway? I wanted to hear where he was going with this.

"So why didn't you say something before?" I asked.

He sighed. "I guess I should have—especially once all my friends started saying what a cute couple you and I made." Was it my imagination, or did his cheeks go a little pink when he said that? The light wasn't too great in the planetarium, so it was hard to tell. "But as an artist, I just felt like I had to follow through on the whole mystery muse thing, you know?"

"I guess," I said. "It *is* a pretty awesome song."

"Thanks." He shot me a bashful smile. "Anyway, when Megan came along, she seemed to fit the part and have all the right answers. And I guess by then I was maybe feeling a little desperate thinking I might never find that girl."

"So you decided she was The One."

"Pretty much." He shot me a sidelong look. "At least until yesterday."

"Yesterday?"

"At the mall. Spending all that time with you, having a great time—well, I was starting to wonder if I was making a mistake. If maybe Planetarium Girl wasn't The One after all."

My breath caught in my throat. "Really? Then why . . ."

"I already had these plans with Megan. And I was still kind of stuck on the muse thing, too. And maybe what I was feeling for you sort of, you know, scared me a little." He gave an adorable little sheepish half smile at that. "So here I am, feeling completely stupid." He reached out and took my hand, squeezing it. "I was being stupid all along. It shouldn't have been so important to track down that girl I met here that day. Maybe I should just be happy that my crazy obsession didn't chase away the coolest girl I've ever met." He hesitated, searching my eyes with his own. "Did it? Will you give me another chance, Lauren?"

I was way too overwhelmed to speak right at that second, even to point out that, duh, I was here, wasn't I? So I just nodded, hoping my eyes told him the rest.

I guess they did, because he smiled, looking happy and relieved. Then he reached into his pocket and pulled out the guitar pick necklace.

"Okay, this might seem kind of weird, since I was about to—well, you know." He laughed softly. "But I really hope you'll accept this. It means a lot to me, and well, I think it'll look perfect on you."

"Oh, wow, I mean, um, wow," I stammered, totally touched by the gesture. "I mean, of course. I love it! Thanks."

Okay, I never claimed to be a poet or anything. But Riley didn't seem to mind. I turned my back and held up my hair. He fastened the chain around my neck, letting his hands linger on my shoulders for a second.

My heart was pounding as I turned around to face him again, touching the guitar pick nestled at my throat. He stared at me. His hands reached for me . . .

The lights cut out. Startled, I let out a

yelp and leaped forward—right into Riley's arms.

He had jumped a little too, but was already laughing. "Whoa," he whispered to me in the dark. "We should stop meeting like this!"

I started laughing, too. Was fate a crazy thing or what? "Tell me about it!" I exclaimed softly. Above us, there was a sudden explosion of light and sound.

We were both still laughing when his lips found mine. My eyes fluttered shut, and I saw stars, even though I wasn't looking up at the planetarium screen. Kissing him felt like swirling through the galaxy without a spaceship. Or maybe not exactly like that. But it did leave me breathless and a little dizzy. And I knew this had to be the most romantic moment in the history of the universe. You know, the one currently expanding right over our heads.

Finally, we came up for air. But he kept holding me, rocking me softly back and forth. I felt his breath tickle my ear as he started to sing to me. It was the song—*my* song. I was so starry-eyed by all that was happening that I thought I might burst with joy. . . .

"Pardon me!" a stern voice hissed from somewhere behind Riley's right shoulder. A second later a tiny but surprisingly strong flashlight beam shot into my eyes, nearly blinding me. "Do you mind? What do you two lovebirds think this is?"

The flashlight spun around to focus on Riley, allowing me to see the face behind it. I gasped. It was her! The very same Stern Scientist Lady who'd caught us together on that fateful day almost two weeks earlier!

"Um, sorry?" Riley was stammering. "We didn't mean—"

"I can't believe it!" the woman cut him off, sounding surprised and disgusted. The flashlight flickered from his face to mine and back again. "*You* two? *Again*? Ugh! I give up!"

She spun on her heel and stomped off into the dark, muttering to herself. Her tiny flashlight lit the way.

Just then a supernova exploded up on the screen. Or something bright happened, anyway. I wasn't looking up; I was watching Riley's eyes widen with amazement.

"So it really was . . . ," he began.

I laughed, pulling him toward me and kissing him again before he could finish. What did it matter? The important thing wasn't him knowing I was the real Planetarium Girl. It was that we were finally together.

Just as I'd imagined at first sight.

About the Author

Catherine Hapka has written more than one hundred and fifty books for children and young adults. In addition to reading and writing, she enjoys horseback riding, animals of all kinds, gardening, music, and traveling. She lives on a small farm in Chester County, Pennsylvania, with a couple of horses, three goats, a small flock of chickens, and too many cats.

LOL at this sneak peek of

Language of Love
By Deborah Reber

A new Romantic Comedy from Simon Pulse

★

How did I get myself into this mess? I stared up at the ceiling looking for an answer. Of course, I knew it wasn't up there. In fact, I already knew the culprit behind my predicament was none other than Molly Harris, my BIF. In Molly's case, BIF stood for "bad influence friend"—the friend who gets you to do all kinds of things you wouldn't normally do but do anyway because that friend holds some sort of voodoo power over you.

To further complicate matters, Molly was my BFF, too. We'd been friends forever, or at least as far back as second grade, when Molly moved onto my block and I had an instant ally in my very testosterone-filled neighborhood. There were boys to the left, boys to the right, and one particularly annoying little boy in the bedroom next to mine.

Molly had me at hello with her shiny blond hair, cornflower blue mischievous eyes, a grin that makes you believe anything is possible, and a confidence that says she'd be president someday if it weren't for the countless scandals she's bound to have a hand in between now and thirty. We'd been through it all together over the years, and though she could certainly be a bit, shall we say, self-involved, at her core Molly was a good person. When it came down to it, I knew she'd always be there for me.

To be fair, Molly didn't get me into this mess alone. In fact, I actually started it. After all, I'm the one who decided impersonating a Hungarian national was a good idea. But I was just having fun. This? This situation I'm in now? Not fun. *Definitely* not fun.

It all started today after school. I met up with Molly at her locker, where she was pulling on her raincoat and reapplying her lipstick, and we figured out a plan for the rest of the day. As usual, Molly's mom was on a business trip—Hong Kong or Tokyo (it's hard to keep track)—and her step-dad wouldn't be home until at least eight o'clock. The plan was to hang out at Molly's house, get some Thai takeout, and catch up on a backlog of seriously good reality TV.

We hopped on the number four bus for the first leg of our journey to Molly's neighborhood of Wallingford, which she'd moved to right after her parents' divorce in fourth grade. The bus was packed, so we squeezed into the rear, claiming a tiny piece of real estate for ourselves and our overstuffed backpacks. We added to the hot air fogging up the bus windows by trading horror stories from the school day—Molly's uncomfortable standoff with a substitute in gym (Molly refused to wear her swim cap) and my continuing inability to bring up my cultural studies grade.

By the time we stepped off the bus at Virginia and Third, I was sure we'd been teleported to the Gulf of Mexico during hurricane season. Having lived in Seattle our whole lives, we were more than used to the rain. And like every other Seattleite, we never carried umbrellas, the thinking being there was no storm that couldn't be weathered with a decent raincoat and a pair of Wellies. Except for, apparently, today. And since we had ten minutes until our bus connection, we decided to seek refuge in the corner Starbucks. The added bonus? *Caffeine.*

As we basked in the warmth and con-
templated the assorted goodies on display
while we waited to order, Molly brought up
my cultural studies grade again. "What's
up with that, anyway?" she probed, shifting
my attention from sugar cookies back to my
bleak academic reality.

"I have no idea. I just don't get how Ms.
Kendall can be such a cool person in real
life, yet such a tyrant of a teacher."

"She must be on some sort of power
trip," Molly mused.

"Yeah, well, I wish she'd get over it
already. If I don't kick butt on this last unit
on Eastern European history, I'm going to
get a D." My voice sank. We both knew
what that meant. I had 99.9 percent convinced my parents to let me go to Europe
with Molly and her mom this summer, but
they told me I had to score Bs or higher in all
my classes. We'd made big plans . . . Paris,
London, Madrid. The fate of my unstamped
passport lay in Ms. Kendall's finely manicured hands.

"I just don't know what else I can do—I
turn in all my homework, I study for the
tests," I rambled on. "You know, I bet
someone who's actually *from* Eastern Europe

couldn't even get a B in her class."

"Um . . . isn't your dad Hungarian, Janna?" Molly asked.

"Well . . . yeah."

"So doesn't that make *you* Eastern European?"

"Kind of, I guess. But I'm talking about someone who's *from* from Eastern Europe. As in, just off the boat," I explained.

I started speaking in an Eastern European accent. "I'm sorry. Which countries are former Eastern Bloc again? France? Mexico? *Alaska?*"

Molly giggled, egging me on.

"Please tell me why zis communism so bad?" I continued, laying it on thick. "And does zis Iron Curtain I hear of come in different fabrics?"

I was on a roll by the time we reached the front of the line and ordered our lattes with fat-free soy, plus a caramel marshmallow thingy for me (I'm a slave to sugar). Molly snagged a tiny table by the window so we could watch for the bus while waiting for our drinks. We had just dumped our bags on the floor and sat down when two boys—two very *cute* boys, I might add— walked up.

Now, it's not all that unusual for random guys to hit on us, or more specifically, on Molly. It's that whole blond, blue-eyed, mischievous smile thing. Plainly put, most members of the male species are drawn to Molly like dogs to a bone. Me? I was pretty much used to my place in our friendship. I was the classic sidekick—the best friend who tries to act as if it's not painfully obvious to everyone that she's nothing more than an accessory to the main attraction. It's not that I'm ugly. I have nice enough honey eyes that come close to matching my light brown wavy hair. And I've even been told I have a warm smile. But put me next to Molly and I've got "plain Jane" (or "plain Janna") written all over me. And that's generally okay by me.

Today, however, was different. First off, these guys didn't come across as your typical supercool guys with heaps of attitude who thought they were all that like the ones who usually hit on us (I mean on Molly). Cute? Yes. But more in a boy-next-door-tussled-hair way as opposed to leading-man-chiseled-cheekbones-six-pack-abs way. For whatever reason, something about them was different enough to make us take notice.

But the *real* difference? Today *I* was the one being hit on.

"Hi there," cute boy number one said.

Having just shoved my entire caramel treat into my mouth, I remained mute and wide-eyed as Molly flashed him a winning smile.

"Well, hi there," she answered flirtatiously.

But the boy, dressed in an army jacket, jeans, and black Converse, flung his hair out of his eyes Zac Efron style and stayed focused on me. Caught off guard, I continued chewing my caramel marshmallow in slow motion, in part because it was sticking to my teeth (perhaps I should have taken a bite instead of eating it whole?) and in part because I hadn't a clue as to what to say.

"I couldn't help but notice your accent," he went on. "So, what country are you from, anyway?"

What *country* was I from? I squinted in confusion.

"Your accent?" he continued. "I overheard you talking before. Wait, let me guess. Somewhere in Eastern Europe? Russia?"

Realizing the source of the misunderstanding, I finished swallowing the caramel and was about to set the record straight when Molly blurted out, "This is Janna! She's an exchange student from Hungary!"

I faced Molly with a look of quiet panic. She returned my gaze with a ridiculously big smile and that damn twinkle in her eye that I'm powerless to resist.

"Hungary? That's so cool!" He was clearly impressed with my apparent heritage. "I'm Julian, by the way. And this is Spence." He motioned to cute boy number two behind him.

I froze. I was at a crossroads and I had to choose a path. I could turn Molly's declaration into a joke and admit I'd never been east of the Rockies, or I could succumb to the message Molly was sending me telepathically (and with several strategically placed kicks under the table). And then in a split second, fueled by unfamiliar cute boy attention, adrenaline, and little else, it was done.

"Sank you," I responded in my most authentic Hungarian accent, which, come to think of it, I'm not sure I've actually even heard before. "I like America veddy much," I added for good measure.

Julian smiled. "I dig the accent," he said. "Where do you girls go to school?"

I sank into my chair and let Molly do the talking, too shocked I was actually going along with the ruse to say a word. I felt slightly guilty about the whole thing, but there was no turning back. Molly was already in full flirtation mode with Spence, and, if I'm being completely honest, the fact that foreign intrigue had magically made me more appealing to at least one very cute member of the opposite sex prompted me to keep my mouth shut. By the time our bus pulled up five minutes later, cell phone digits had been exchanged and we'd planned to connect at a club Friday night.

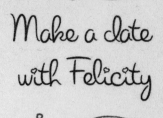

Make a date
with Felicity

and look for:

From Simon Pulse ♥ Published by Simon & Schuster

Want to hear what the Romantic Comedies authors are doing when they are not writing books?

Check out
PulseRoCom.com
to see the authors blogging together, plus get sneak peeks of upcoming titles!

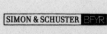